Dark Talent

By

Chad Di Lillo

This book is a work of fiction. Names, characters, businesses, organizations, places, events, and incidents are the product of the author's imagination. While some references may resemble actual names, characters, businesses, organizations or places, the events detailed, and dialogue are for entertainment purposes only.

Copyright © 2019 by Chad Di Lillo

Edited by Leslie Wells
Cover design by Chad Di Lillo
Cover photograph by Jeff Southwick, Single Man Studios
Cover model, Cori Hailmann

This book is dedicated to Drew, Kenzie, and Hannah. Each one of you gives me inspiration and guidance in this life to do what is right and to make right what was wrong. You give me the strength, desire, and willingness to continue writing even when no one is reading. You are my reason. I love you.

Love, Dad

"Revenge is only sweet if you are present to see it. Revenge is destiny that will manifest itself only through training and constant rigor in the minds of the youth. You were born for destine; to seek the ultimate and final revenge."

-    Mary Rothwell

Chapter One

"Can I help you Mrs. Rothwell?"

"I am here to see Sheriff Stanley."

"Is he expecting you?"

"My husband is missing. He was murdered and I need to talk to the sheriff, now." Replied Mary Rothwell.

Deputy Robertson walked Mary down the hall to Stan Stanley's office. Mary was with her young daughter, as they made their way into the office.

"Close the door Mrs. Rothwell. Now how can I help you?"

"I have been calling and no one has called me back, so I came down. My husband Peter, was murdered by Aaron Rocklin."

There was a long, uncomfortable silence that filled the air. Sheriff Stanley, who was sitting behind his big oak desk, displayed no emotion. He was scared. Mary was standing in front of the desk, looking into his eyes.

"Mrs. Rothwell, please sit down. The accusation you are making against Mr. Rocklin, is serious. Do you have any proof or evidence of this?"

Taking a seat in one of the two big chairs in front of the desk, Mary responded.

"Sheriff, Aaron Rocklin killed my husband. What are you going to do about it?"

"Mary, may I call you Mary?"

"Yes"

"Mary, do you even know the Rocklin's? Do you know who they are?"

Mary sat back in the chair and looked over at her

daughter who was reading a book. She looked back at Sheriff Stanley.

"Stan, may I call you Stan?"

"Yes Mary, you can call me Stan."

"Stan, we moved here because of Aaron and Sandy. We are, or we were friends. I know them very well."

"So, you understand why I am asking, right? They are not just your typical business owners. They are both very well respected in this town and they know 'the right people', if you understand where I am coming from. You can't come into this office and make an accusation of murder, unless you have some kind of proof. Do you have any proof?"

"No, I do not have any hard proof. I know they had something to do with his disappearance."

With a puzzled look, Sheriff Stanley, look at the

little girl sitting beside her mother.

"Mary, where is your husband?"

"He is dead, murdered."

"Is he missing, did he disappear, or was he murdered? And you have the body, right?"

"No, I do not have the body, we have not heard from him in 2 days."

Standing up, Sheriff Stanley walked slowly towards the door.

"Mary, my suggestion to you would be to file a missing persons claim. We can then put the word out of his disappearance and can have deputies be on the lookout for your husband."

Mary stood up and grabbed her daughter's hand, glaring at the sheriff.

"Sheriff, my husband is NOT fucking missing, he is dead. Do your fucking job."

And Mary Rothwell grabbed the door handle and threw the door open, slamming it into the wall, uttering obscenities under her breath as she walked out of the police station.

****

He was not a tall man. His body was slender but defined. He had the look of someone who hit the gym several times a week but had not actually picked up a weight in years, he had good genes. His hair was short and black, graying a little around the edges, exquisitely debonair. The goatee was short, tapered around the mouth with a little salt and pepper.

Charlie looked once again in the mirror and ran his fingers through his hair with a little product. With a slight grin, he was ready.

Charlie got his hair cut at 10:30 on the second Tuesday of the month, at the same place by the same person. Mollie had been cutting his hair for over ten years. She was the owner of *Inspire*, a private salon. A masseuse worked there by appointment only, and there was a separate room off the back that played relaxing music, with the smell of fresh lavender during therapy sessions and water infused with cucumber sitting in the corner. It was a private salon, meaning you had to pay a membership fee just to walk into the place. What is this world coming to, when you must be a "member" just to get your hair cut, fucking ridiculous, but Charlie wasn't bothered by the cost. It was the quality, service, and exclusivity he desired.

Today, he was dressed in a custom-made Tom Ford Windsor three-piece charcoal suit and an embroidered shirt with his initials on the collar, "CAR":

Charles A. Rocklin. His tie, Brioni and socks that never matched anything. His sock collection was anything but simple. His sock collection was something to be found in the Smithsonian. Charlie did not own a solid-colored pair of socks; everything was bright and colorful. He wore a new pair of Christian Louboutin dress shoes that had finally arrived after four months, making this his twelfth pair of Louboutin shoes. Platinum cuff links and a tie rope. Brian made sure that everything in Charlie's closet was pressed and ready to be worn. Brian took good care of Charlie when he was home. Charlie was the kind of man that when he walked into a place, all eyes would be on him, and that was the plan. He created the appeal. This was his business; he needed to always be the first-person people saw and the only person they remembered.

"The first impression is the only impression," he

would often say.

On the outside, he had on a smile, or at least that is what he wanted one to think. Charlie Rocklin was the owner and president of Rocklin and Roll Investments, Inc.

The company was started nine years ago with a bank loan of $200,000 and one hundred clients, most of them family and close friends. Charlie was sick of working for other people and making *them* money, so he decided to make a change. Risky yes, but with high risk came the potential of high reward. Of course, there were times of despair and struggling to pay rent or even make the payroll. As the economy slowly came out of the recession in June of 2009, Charlie began to capitalize through his networking and constant research on the global economy, investments, and stocks. Then again, was there ever a doubt? It was Charlie Fuckin Rocklin.

Arrogant, yes. Confident, yes. Passionate, yes. Sympathetic, not so much.

Charlie liked the allure of Wall Street, and had a gift with investments. What did both of these have in common? The green shit, and lots of it. When Charlie was growing up, his father often talked about their financial planner who managed the bulk of the family money. When Charlie was old enough to truly understand the potential in that market, he never looked back. There was an art to this sort of work. Wall Street was not for everyone, but everyone wanted Wall Street. You could make a decent living playing on Wall Street, but Charlie did not want a "decent" living; he wanted to have it all, he wanted the world and everything in it. *Wall Street, Trading Places, Casino, The Sting, The Godfather*: movies about money, greed, power, respect, and passion. Charlie knew the goal, dream big, go after the whales, and harpoon the fuckers. The weak were destroyed, chewed up, and spit out without a single swallow. The strong survived. Charlie was the Bos Taurus, and he was hung.

Twelve years ago, Charlie started with Dean Witter. This was when Dean Witter was still Dean Witter, until that asshole Morgan Stanley came riding in on his white horse and took control. Charlie quickly became the top producer for Witter in the office, then in the entire state, and soon in the country, earning himself a corner office with a view and relinquishing his rights to the five-by-five cubical he *was* working in. Coming into the office and making cold calls to drum up business was not what Charlie had planned to do for an extended period of time. Everyone must get their feet wet; everyone had to start on the phone, with the dreaded, unsolicited, and annoying cold calls. He did it, and he did it with a smile, passion, dedication, knowing it was just part of his plot. Weekly office huddles of the hottest stocks or tips were shared with the floor. Production numbers were broadcast in public for everyone to see, creating a dangerous level of cutthroat competition against his own peers. Charlie was growing weary of this environment.

Carefully crafting a business plan and aligning his clientele, he took the inevitable plunge of going out on his own and creating a corporation. This was four years in the making, and Charlie learned a great deal from the managing broker in the office. The time had come for Charlie to break free and create something he called his own. Dean Witter and their brokers could focus on the cold calls and $1,000 trades, but Charlie had bigger goals to conquer. The short-term plan was to focus on the higher end of the financial ladder. In his seminars, he would repeat the following: "You will only make as much as your clients make," and when you were dealing with investments, nothing could be closer to the truth. You want to deal with buying and selling penny stocks, go for it. You want to spend your time selling a few hundred shares of Apple, go for it. Charlie spent his time buying and selling Berkshire Hathaway. Fuck Apple!

Rocklin and Roll Investments: what a cool fucking name, right? Charlie liked to get in and get out, always on the move, "rock and roll." Frank "the Enforcer" Nitti would have been proud. Know your objective, see your objective, and get your objective. Done, Next. No need to talk about the weather, or how the Bears did last weekend, that was for amateurs who were happy making a couple hundred thousand a year. Not to say Charlie didn't get to know his clients or spend time with them, but there IS one word in there that you MUST pay attention to: "client." Know your client, be your client. If your client knows you, they will trust you. Charlie has built his business on trust. Being incorporated for a little over eight years, Rocklin and Roll Investments made number one on the Wall Street Journal's list of hottest investment firms in the country, and HAS remained in the top five ever since. No money was ever spent on advertising; word of mouth and personal referrals were his single source of new clients. Being a client of Charlie Rocklin was not a right; it was a privilege.

His clients were people he knew well. And if he did not know them, he got to know them, and only then did they become clients. When your hourly rate is $10,000, you needed to be someone if meeting with Charlie. Building relationships was the priority, followed very closely by money, but not money alone.

Money was damned special – it created the world in

which we lived; it was the means to live – but *money*

alone wasn't enough to become a client of Charlie

Rocklin.

Two years ago, Charlie met with Rick Rogers, an

internet pioneer who had just become one of the

youngest billionaires in the world simply by buying up

domain names and selling them. The World Wide Web

was taking off, and thousands upon thousands of

companies, business and individuals were registering

domains. Rick predicted the impact of this new media

and began registering every name he could think of.

Some of these were Bank of America, Tiffany & Co, Ford

Motor Company, and Warner Brother's. Rick would

register the name for five years at $20 a year, or $100 for

the five years. Then when one of the companies came to

him to purchase the domain, he sold it to them for millions. They did not negotiate and only asked one question; who should we write this check to?

The meeting was arranged by the late Victor Shallows, who was a very close friend. Charlie flew to Southern California on a Thursday, and landed at 9:20 in the morning. Rick was 40 minutes late to their meeting. Rather than leaving and catching his jet back home, Charlie waited. When Rick did finally show up, Charlie met him in the doorway, greeting him with a handshake, said, "Great to meet you Rick, Charlie Rocklin," and walked out to his waiting car that took him straight to his plane. He was home by noon. There were no other words spoken and no other thoughts crossed Charlie's mind. Rick called Charlie several times, but never got a returned call back. If you are going to be late, you should let Charlie know. Rick never became a client, no matter who referred him. He hadn't earned the privilege.

For the first seven years, Charlie never went home before midnight. He was up at 4:00 in the morning, going through files, reading emails, working on client plans, studying company financials, and scheduling meetings. Nothing else in his life even came close to his work. Then, something happened. All the long hours, all the flights, and all the meetings, it happened almost overnight. His phone began to ring, and the calls were not from potential or current clients, but the media. Magazines, literary agents, book publishers; you name it. Everyone wanted some of Charlie. Charlie soon found another niche: speaking engagements. People and corporations would pay hundreds of thousands of dollars, just to hear what he had to say. Charlie had now achieved the leisure of working part-time and lecturing part-time. Due to articles and interviews in various business publications and online combined with his successful rate of return, companies all over the world not only wanted to be clients, but wanted him to come talk to their board or executive leaders, and they paid whatever the asking price was. Charlie gave lectures at universities, workshops, inaugurations, and company meetings. He may not have been familiar with every type of business in the world, but there was one thing that all businesses have in common, and that was to make a profit. Increase revenue, increase productivity, decrease expenses; this is something Charlie was an expert in. Making the shareholders happy was a specialty Charlie had mastered over the past decade. It was amazingly simple: make a product, create a demand, sell it for more than it costs to make. Sure, there are logistics to accomplishing this, and your product has to have the right timing, but

that is why Charlie made close to $250 million last year.

Of course, not all years were that lucrative, but Charlie

has never had a bad year. His average take home, over

the past 4 years was just over 200 million a year.

Charlie was 44 and unmarried, nor had he ever

been married. Charlie never had time to settle down

with anyone. He was really never interested in meeting

women because he wanted to concentrate on business.

From the moment he passed the series 7 and 66, there

was only one plan. There would be plenty of time to

meet women or go on dates, but for now he was focused

on securing his future, his legacy. He'd had several

girlfriends, but nothing you would call a "serious"

relationship. He was content with the life he was

leading. Money was something that Charlie never

wanted to have to worry about. If Charlie stopped

working altogether, he would never have to worry about supporting the life he'd created. When you have a net worth of $5 billion, you worry more about preservation than accumulation. Did he have to work? No, but he breathed investments, stocks, and portfolios. That was his life and that is what gave him passion.

Charlie often was alone, and that was the way he liked it. He was alone in his personal life as well as his business life. Yet, while he may be alone, he was far from being lonely. No one else took meetings with his clients; no one else discussed company financials or proposals, and this was by design. There were no distractions in his life that he did not control or was not in control of. With all the client meetings, travel, and lectures, Charlie was quite used to being alone. He had an office full of paper-pushers, but they kept the office and business afloat. Being alone had its advantages.

There were no partners to confer with; no one to challenge his decisions and no one he had to answer to, except for his clients.

Charlie was at a point where he genuinely enjoyed going into the office and meeting with clients. He also liked the hectic schedule of traveling all over the country, discussing financial solutions, and being able to share his knowledge and expertise. Yes, it was an ego thing, but Charlie received great satisfaction from seeing the success of his work and how it helped his clients. If you boil it down, his greatest joy was seeing his work prosper, watching his clients achieve what they hired him to do. Of course, he needed his clients to be successful if he wanted to be successful. Like Jay Gatsby, he threw grand parties with hundreds of people, and gave money to his favorite charities. He liked to share his wealth with those around him. He was always the first one in and the first to leave and he paid for everything. He spent money on great houses and exotic cars. His newest acquisition was a red 1989 Aston Martin Vantage Volante. There were only 22 in existence in the world, built specifically for the 'Prince of Wales' royal family. He only drove her on Fridays to keep the miles low. Sometimes he would take her out on the weekends, but only if the weather was nice enough to put the top down and enjoy the wind in his hair. Among his other prized automotive possessions were a 1992 Lamborghini LM002, a 1997 Ferrari Testarossa, and a 1990 Vector. He had a 40,000-square-foot garage built to house his collection of cars. Cars became a passion for Charlie; some might even call it obsession. This was his one true love.

The people who worked for Charlie had stayed with him since he left Dean Witter. They were his family. He treated them with respect, and gave them the

credit they deserved. He gave each one a bonus every

month, based on his profits. And at the end of the year,

he flew them and their families to Hawaii for the

company's Christmas party. One week, completely paid

for, with no mention of work.

"You have made me what I am, and I will never

forget that. You will continue to grow <u>with</u> me, not by

me," he would say each year. He would often say in

interviews that of course people come to work to get

paid, but if you reward your employees, and treat them

well, they will exceed their potential and have a vested

interest in what they do and who they do it for. Respect

and appreciation were core values during office

meetings, and when he was working with other

companies. Forget the daily work tasks, forget the 9-5

mentality; respect and appreciation will always reward

you as an employer.

A typical day in Charlie's life went something like this: make and receive about 200 calls a day; talk to current clients such as Bill Gates, Ted Turner, Lawrence Ellison, former President Obama, Michael Jordan, and Tiger Woods. Charlie would also talk to potential clients, but only if they are referred to him by existing clients. He does not cold call, nor does he accept cold calls. Presidents of companies like IBM, AT&T, and General Motors called for advice or investment transactions; Charlie did not call them. Money was always moving, and money was always being made. If it was a travel week, Charlie would take many of his calls from the car or plane. In between meetings, he would be talking to clients and when he was in a meeting, you never saw his phone. You were paying for him and his undivided attention and that is what you got.

"If it is not moving, we're not moving, so make it move and make some money." Charlie was a rainmaker.

Charlie may have been very busy and on the phone nearly twelve hours out of a thirteen-hour workday, but he always knew where his money was and what it was doing. He never had someone else do something that he could do, with respect to his or his clients' money. He signed every check that went out of the office, initiated every wire transfer, and approved every purchase and investment personally. This certainly made his life more pressured and chaotic, and added a few hours on to each day; but if there was ever a problem, he could only blame himself. He never wanted to go through a struggle with a partner or associate over money or other dealings, so he kept it all simple. Transactions went through one door, and that was his.

Every other Thursday, you could always find Charlie

sitting at his desk late at night, approving all the payroll.

An in-house payroll service prepared the amounts, but

they all required his approval to go live.

Charlie had learned to keep a handle on

everything that went on in his company. Keep things

small, and manageable and always know what is going

on with your own money. Warren Buffett had provided

an invaluable service to Charlie. Warren would often tell

Charlie that he would never regret being too involved.

An example Warren shared several years ago was about

a real estate investor in New York. Worth billions, he

soon became complacent and too relaxed with his

finances, and hired Harvard graduates to take care of

some financial obligations and transactions. After a

while, he noticed that he was losing a lot of money. The

next year, the same investor went from being one of the

top ten richest men in the world, to not even a blip on the chart. After a major house-cleaning and regaining control of all of the financial and personnel transactions, he found himself, once again, a member of the billionaire's club. A hard lesson to learn, but one that Warren reminds himself of every day.

"Never get too comfortable with the way things are. There should be only one door, and you should always have the key," Warren told Charlie.

During his undergrad studies at Stanford University, Charlie took an interest in Psychology. In fact, he even changed his major from Accounting to Psychology. After his first Psych class, he became fascinated by the mind and its capabilities. He focused on Social Psychology and the study of human and social interaction, which would help explain his success with selling and investing, and his behavioral patterns. You know how they say when students in medical school start reading up on the symptoms of a particular disease, they come down with the symptoms they are reading about? That is how it was with Charlie: as he began to read more and more about the mind and the psychological factors in social interaction, he began to develop an anal-retentive mindset, and moved into a slight obsessive-compulsive way of doing things. Which in his case, was a good thing.

Charlie went on to major in Social Psychology and pursue his interest in people's minds, their interactions and why they did certain things. After a very short time, he soon realized that while you can make a living dealing with people's emotions and actions or reactions, he was more attracted back to his (financial) accounting. His background provided the perfect balance for setting up his company and selling himself. He often touched on his education during his lectures and speeches. Charlie never needed the formal Accounting or Math education; that came naturally. He was great with numbers, yet if you asked him how he learned it, he could not say. It just came to him; he was one of those often-envied "numbers" people.

Charlie motivated himself, and he had this ability to motivate everyone he met. He would share personal stories of what seemed to be helpless situations and how he overcame challenges to achieve what he wanted. This is what motivated others. If he saw something he wanted, he would go after it and usually get it. If he saw that you needed or wanted something, he would encourage you until you got it. Debby in the office was getting brochures in the mail for a two-week Caribbean cruise. But because she and her husband just purchased two new cars, they could not afford the cruise. There was nothing wrong with dreaming, though, she thought.

Debby was setting her sights on the cruise within the

next two years, just as she did with the cars. With the

help of Charlie and his motivation (one Friday morning,

Debby came in to work and opened the brochure that

had come the previous week, and as she turned the page

an envelope fell out; as she opened the envelope, she

found two first-class tickets for a two-week cruise to the

Caribbean, along with an itinerary for the flight to

Florida and lodging), Debby was able to go on her

cruise. If you treated him right, he treated you right.

Charlie Rocklin always made dreams come true. Even if

the dream was truly just that, a dream, he would make it

a reality, sparing no cost. He was a true miracle worker

to those who knew him.

There wasn't much more to know about Charlie

Rocklin. That was all there was to know about Charlie

Rocklin - at least all that he wanted anyone to know.

Chapter Two

As the plane landed on the tarmac, the phone began to ring. With slightly blurred vision, Charlie wiped his eyes and glanced at the incoming call, which was from a blocked number. That usually meant an unwanted solicitation or a debt collector. It was too late for one and never a reason for the other, so Charlie answered. There was no one on the other end, no response, but Charlie could hear a minor sound of a person taking a breath. A few minutes later, back in his jacket pocket, his phone rang again, seemingly from the same blocked number. Charlie answered, but not with his usual "This is Charlie". Again, no response after answering, but he could hear the sound of someone opening their mouth as if they needed a drink. Charlie hung up, looked at his phone and placed it in his pocket, once again.

It was late on Friday evening, and Charlie was physically and emotionally exhausted. The kind of exhaustion where you can hardly keep a single thought in your mind, or keep both eyes focused on the same thing. A drunken kind of exhaustion. He had just finished up a weeklong trip to Northern California for his annual visit to the once fleeting computer firm, followed by a quick stopover in Chicago. For the first four days, he conducted a strategy workshop for the senior leaders and executives, and then gave a company-wide lecture on the last day. As with all of Charlie's clients, he makes an annual pilgrimage, in person, to meet with the executives and address any new strategies or changes in existing priorities. Ambrosia was one of Charlie's first big clients years ago. When they first called upon him, the firm had been one of the top-

producing computer firms of the eighties, but had fallen

behind in technology, product satisfaction and outdated

devices, while also running into management problems,

causing their downfall. The two original partners had

left the company to pursue other interests and had sold

off the majority of their shares. On the company's verge

of collapse, the remaining management called Charlie,

who convinced the board to bring back some familiar

faces. Once the two original founders, one being Victor

Shallows, returned to deal with the day-to-day

operations, they called Charlie. Victor and Pete already

had a relationship with Charlie Rocklin, when he was

with Dean Witter.

It was the Ambrosia connection that allowed

Charlie to start his own company. During Charlies first

visit to Ambrosia in Cupertino, he recommended

moving the company from several small office buildings

to a large-scale campus, in an effort to consolidate

overhead and create a "OneAmbrosia" mentality. They

were an exceptionally large organization, but they were

too segregated. At the time, they had a proprietary

computer system, a portable music player and an

outdated mobile phone, but they were lacking further

innovation and had no other products in their pipeline.

Charlie helped correct that. Hardware and software

were not Charlie's forte, but he brought investments,

numbers and ideas that helps transform the out of the

box thinking. As with any "product of the week"

company in technology, a paradigm can switch

overnight. Somewhere out there, someone is training,

and when you meet face-to-face in combat, they will beat

you. Ambrosia was getting complacent. Not moving

quickly enough with advancements in technology, Victor

and Pete needed an outside consultation. For three

entire days, it was Victor, Pete, Charlie, and the Chief

Scientist of the R&D department, locked in a conference

room surrounded by transparent white boards and

smart boards. Every square inch of anything that could

be written on, was occupied. There was no talk of what

was or placing blame, only what could be.

Research and development were out of the scope

of Charlie's expertise, he provided rationale and

optimism from an outside and consumer perspective,

one that the executives were unable to grasp being too

close to operations. Ambrosia had done it before with

their music player and phone. They now needed to

break the mold and come up with something new,

something fresh, and something that had never been

seen before. A reinvention of consumerization. Not that

Charlie was the principal of the new launch that was

about to catapult Ambrosia, but he was the voice of reason, a major financial consultant and voice of the customer. Soon after Charlie finished his first consulting work with Ambrosia, a portable, consumer-based platform was launched. This was a product that the world had not seen before. It was a product you could take with you, search the internet, play games, send emails, and then slide it into the side of your briefcase or put in your purse. The launch was a global event with throngs of consumers waiting in 5-hour lines, just to spend $500.00 on a consumption only device. But Charlie never made the business headlines, he was never even mentioned. And that was by design.

He'd always been a "behind the scenes" kind of guy. As a consumer, you are not aware of what happens behind those executive doors. Even when you think an organization is doing well, they are really scrambling,

and that is when they call Charlie. With Apple, it
worked before, and it worked again. Debt consolidation,
restructuring, simplifying the supply chain, investments,
capital, strategy, mindfulness, calculated risks and
looking at the red and black; this is what Charlie brings
to the table.

Before he even agrees to accept a job of
consulting, Charlie looks at the complete financials of a
company since inception. Charlie then prepares a
preliminary spreadsheet and a roadmap of where the
company has been, versus where it is going, and what it
will take to get there. Additionally, he draws
comparisons with other companies with similar product
lines and industry, detailing out financials, strategic
plans, and costs to achieve these. Only then will Charlie
consider taking on the project or decide to pass.
Sometimes, even if Charlie decides to take on a new

client or project, the company decides to pass. Why pass

on Charlie? The cost. Green shit. $500,000, and this is

just a retainer.   This does not include travel, lodging, or

meals. Again, this is simply a retainer fee. Charlie will

make his preliminary presentation, touching on his ideas

as well as the realities of the company's situation. He

will then deliver it to the CEO and President, then to the

rest of the Board of Directors, if necessary, for majority

approval. If the company decides to adopt Charlie's

ideas and recommendations, Charlie presents them with

a detailed script of what needs to be done to improve the

organization, as he did in Chicago, along with a bound

book of policies and procedures. He uses their existing

manuals as a base for his new and revised manual.

Charlie then becomes one with the company. He takes

an office onsite, and begins to work with the internal

partners, finance, and operations, to get a hands-on

understanding of how the company operates; not how the president *thinks* it operates. Charlie has seven employees, and he chooses a staff of three for every new project. Within four weeks, Charlie will have concluded his efforts and will make the final presentation.

With the company in Chicago, Charlie added an additional 50 pages of new policies and procedures. Often, he added 75 pages of new information, depending on the complexity of what he wanted to implement. Charlie is not a cheap hire; depending on the size of the company and their current financial market position, fees may vary. On this deal, the one from Chicago, Charlie made roughly $21 million for four months of work, and this was an average payday for him.

In addition to the retainer fee, and not including other expenses, Charlie receives 45 percent of the first-year gross sales from the time his program is put into place. The percentage is so high because Charlie does not receive earnings after that first year. He could draw it out over a couple of years, or even negotiate a percentage of the business, but he has found it more profitable to collect money during that first year since statistically, sales begin to drop after that. Once a new idea is introduced, it naturally draws interest to the organization. Consumers notice the "new" and forget the "old". As people get to know the new idea, however, the novelty wears off, or competition has caught up, or the company begins to idle. By this time, Charlie has collected his fee and is on to the next company.

During the initial review, Charlie does not take on the project unless he is confident that (1) there is a viable effort the company is willing to put in; (2) the company can be profitable and (3) his efforts will actually make a difference. The results and rewards are his fees and first year commissions, but unless Charlie

feels there is going to be a profitable return, on both

sides, he will respectfully decline. One other

characteristic that sets Charlie apart from other

consultants is that he makes himself available to his

existing clients at no charge, for life. Once you are a

client, you remain a client, unless you sever the

relationship; then there is no turning back. You only get

one chance. Charlie is a mentor and friend you do not

want to lose. Just like with his employees, you treat him

right, and he will treat you very well.

Charlie's plane from Chicago had just landed,

and he was walking to his car parked in his hangar.

Tired and ready to go home and relax, Charlie loved

living ten miles from the airport. That was the nice thing

about living in Lake Tahoe. Everything was relatively

close to his house and office. As he loaded his bags into

the car, he noticed a note on his windshield. He walked

around to the passenger side to get a better look. He

glanced around the hangar, but it was dark and quiet.

There were no other cars, and no other people. He also

turned his attention to the closed wrought iron gate that

could only be opened by a remote, that was in his car.

The only glimmer of light was from the fluorescent bulb

over his car, flickering as if it was draining of energy and

ready to call it a night. As he bent over the hood, he

noticed that the note was held in place with a chewed

piece of gum. A chill ran up his spine and

simultaneously down his legs; he could feel the goose

bumps forming.

Charlie removed the note from the windshield,

gum and all, and opened it. It read: *"Would you be hot if*

you were in the hot and boiling sun all day, think you could

survive?"

After reading the message twice, he had no idea what to make of it. Too tired to even try, he crumpled up the note, threw it onto the passenger seat, and started his car. Driving through the gate, Charlie stopped to watch it close from his rearview mirror. More cautious than normal, he slowly drove out of the airport, exhausted but wide eyed as he drove on CA-28 toward his house. It was two in the morning, no one else was on the road, and all he wanted to do was be home.

Waiting for his security gate to open, Charlie looked around once more and stared into the darkness, he saw nothing. The gate can only be opened from the outside with a digital remote control. Every time the button is pushed to open the gate, it generates a new five-digit pass code, always different than the time before. There is also a keypad on the outside of the gate that automatically creates a new entry code every 24 hours. This code is then transmitted to a secure file share that is only accessible by a two-factor authentication. Charlie and Brian are the only ones authorized to access the file share. Every time the file share is accessed, it sends Charlie a notification. When you are leaving the property, once a vehicle hits the infrared light towards the bottom of the drive, the gate opens. It cannot be activated by a person or by walking into the infrared light; only a car can trigger the gate to open, from the inside. The only other option of opening the gate is from inside the mud room of the house. Closed circuit cameras are located on the outside of the gate, at the bottom of the driveway to see who is leaving and inside the mud room. No one enters the estate without Charlie or Brian knowing. Charlie and Brian both receive new, different codes every 24 hours and Charlie is notified what code is assigned to Brian, but

Brian does not have access to Charlie's code.

Once he was inside his house, he did not bother to unpack. He just jumped into a quick shower to get the smell of Chicago off him and fell face-first on his massive California King.

Awakened by the glaring sun through the two skylights above his bed, he saw that it was 6:00 a.m. It was Saturday. A quick trip to the office was in order since he had not been there all week. He went in to sign three checks, pay some bills, and validate a few retainers that had been wired the night before. By 11:00 a.m. his work was done. Standing next to his desk and looking out his window at a tranquil Lake Tahoe, running his hands through his hair, Charlie had a smile on his face, shaking his head as though he knew he lived well. He placed the signed checks on his secretary's desk, with delivery instructions. He itemized the retainers in a spreadsheet, totaling just under $20 million, and left a

note for her to disburse the funds in various accounts

when she returned on Monday. He closed the door to

his office and set the alarm. Charlie and his secretary

were the only ones with the codes to disarm the alarm.

He had a unique code that only he knew, and his

secretary had her own unique code. The office suite also

had an alarm that he set as he left for the day. All entries

into the alarm system were monitored, so he could tell

when and at what times the offices were entered. This

was not because Charlie doesn't trust his secretary or his

staff, but simply that he was overly careful about his

business.

As he pushed the down arrow for the elevator,

Charlie's phone rang. Taking it out of his pocket, he saw

it was from a blocked number. He did not answer this

time. Just as he slipped the phone into his pocket, the

elevator doors opened and Charlie looked up, then

abruptly stopped. It was Saturday and he was in a

private elevator, accessed only by a passcode, but he was

not alone.

"Hello?" he said in a questioning tone to a lady

with a large hat and sunglasses, standing in the back

corner. The dress was short, red with white lace trim,

and the hat was big enough to cover two heads. It was

pulled down low in front to hide her face. This was

more than a little perplexing, considering that he and his

secretary were the only ones with passcodes to access the

elevator. The elevator led directly into the lobby of his

company. Only during normal business hours was the

penthouse suite accessible without the code. With a hint

of concern, Charlie got in the elevator, smiled at the lady,

and pushed the button for Level 1 parking. There were

no other buttons lit on the panel. Charlie got chills and

glanced, at the strange figure standing in the corner. She

did not look up.

The elevator came to a stop at Level 1, and

Charlie waited for the doors to open. As he walked off

the elevator, the mysterious lady in the red dress

followed. Walking toward his car, the only one in the

lot, parked in the corner in his reserved space, he could

hear the sound of heels clicking on the concrete behind

him. Now his attention was piqued; who the fuck was

she? He needed to know what this person was doing

and what she wanted. Charlie was not afraid, but more

puzzled. The sound of clicking heels dissipated, then

disappeared. Turning around abruptly to ask if he could

help her, he found that he was talking to himself. She

was gone.

Charlie stood there, looked around. He glanced

at the empty elevator that was closing and turned back

towards his car. The garage was empty, the sound of silence was deafening. The lady had vanished. Charlie walked a little faster to his car, unlocked the door with the remote, and quickly drove off.

The weather was perfect on this particular Saturday. Nothing can clear the mind like a cool wind blowing through your hair while looking at Tahoe blue water. He pushed a button, and the electric top rolled down to expose the sun, the fresh air with a hint of pine, and the crystal blue surrounding view. Charlie knew of only one place that would help him take his mind off the mysterious lady, and one person who would listen.

With the sun reflecting off his sunglasses, Charlie reached for his phone. He continued down Highway 28 toward his sanctuary, Rotchedo's Restaurant and Bar, owned by Frankie Rotchedo, one of Charlie's oldest and closest confidants. Frankie was the only person who would tell Charlie what he needed to know, not what he

wanted to hear. A person with all heart, yet brutally

honest, he had been there through the tears and the

celebrations. Rotchedo's was the "Cheers" of Lake

Tahoe, the neighborhood bar and grill, if you were lucky

enough to get a table. Charlie was there at least twice a

week, whether it to dine in or take out. It was truly his

asylum. A table overlooking the lake had a permanent

reserved sign, just for him.

Rotchedo's sat right on Tahoe's North shore,

along Highway 28 in Tahoe City. Close enough to

everything, but far enough from the neon lights of the

South shore casinos. Well known for its decor and lake

setting, as well as its food, its well-to-do customers could

eat in the main house, or out on the floating pier during

the summer months. The main house was an old

mansion that had been vacant for a decade before

Frankie purchased it and renovated the entire interior and exterior. Frankie, a business major in college, opened Rotchedo's within a year of graduating Stanford. On any given evening, the restaurant had a line of people waiting to get a table, and those were the ones who had reservations.

Frankie was a longtime pal of Charlie's. They attended the same boarding school, grew up together, and roomed together at college. Frankie came from a family with very old money: salt of the Earth, turn-of-the-century, fucking old. Money that started being made in the early 1800's by Frankie's ancestors. Frankie's grandfather, Robert, went to school with Rockefeller, Morgan, and Steel from the late 1800's and when those men needed money, they called Robert.

By the time Frankie was old enough to understand the concept of money, he had inherited $125 million from his great-grandfather, and he was one of five great-grandchildren. Frankie did not need to work, but he chose to go to school and double major in Business Accounting and Restaurant Management. He followed his passion and dream of owning his own restaurant. He worked all through school, and never took advantage of his money or the clout it provided: he lived with Charlie in a two-bedroom, run-down shithole all through college. He even drove a 10-year-old Oldsmobile. The damn piece of shit only started half the time, and Robert had to bum rides from Charlie. Yet he had so much money, he had accounts with every bank in town.

When Charlie and Frankie met at St. Francis boarding school at the age of 13, both had a solid family foundation. The boarding school required the parents to partake in at least 20 hours per year of volunteer time to help with school activities. This ensured a family

relationship to promote solidarity. School activities

included such tasks as helping in the classroom grading

papers, being a teacher's aide for the day, or

administrative office duties like filing or answering the

phone. One volunteering activity not found at St.

Francis is in the cafeteria. Every day of the week was

catered by a different fine dining restaurant. Charlie and

Frankie's mothers met in the classroom. From there, it

seemed the boys were destined to become friends. You

often hear about young adults following the love of their

life as they go to school or start their professional careers,

but rarely do you hear about friends doing this.

Frankie's mother and father, Rose and Robert, Jr., had a

house on 25 acres up in the hills of West Virginia.

Charlie's parents, Sandra and Aaron, had a house built

on the parcel of land next to the Rotchedos. They had 25

acres as well. Once Charlie's parents decided to move to Nevada in the '50s, the Rotchedos followed. They packed up and moved out West, together. Both purchased land and built homes in Las Vegas, next door to one another.

The year was 1956, and Las Vegas was still a place primarily owned and operated by the mob. Vegas was a place where in '56, you fucked with no one, unless you were looking to get fucked yourself, and we are not talking about prostitution. You could be protected, but at any time, you may be called upon to return the favor, and if called, there was only one right response. This was a place where you could leave your doors and windows open 24 hours a day, and know that when you got home at night, the TV and phone would still be there. Unless, of course, you were on the other side of the mob; then it was best if you just left. The crime rate was controlled, just one of the advantages of the different mob families having influence over Vegas. In 1956, Las Vegas was becoming the gambling mecca of the World. Vegas was relatively small with only a handful of casinos in the middle of the desert: El Rancho, Thunderbird, Desert Inn, Sahara, Riviera, and the Dunes. They were brought to reality with mafia money and by men who saw something in Vegas that no one else did. These men took a chance and envisioned a dream that transformed Vegas to what it is today. Celebrities were often invited to stay and were used to drawing in traffic. It was not uncommon to find Sinatra at a blackjack table at 1:00 in the morning, drinking scotch on the rocks. Nor was it uncommon for frequent visitors to be called by their names and extended offers of "encouragement" to play in the casinos. Unlike today, Vegas was a simple, well-organized, orchestrated show. If you got a bad hand dealt to you, you lost. You did not make a fuss or a scene, because if you did, you would not be returning. And not just returning to the hotel; you would not be returning, period. Life and times were good to those who were good in return. Those who stayed loyal were rewarded, and those who were not, were shown the way out of town or buried somewhere in the desert. And sometimes, you did not have a choice; it was chosen for you.

The Rocklins moved to Nevada for one reason: they also saw an opportunity. Every previous summer leading up to 1956, Sandra and Aaron had spent three months in the desert, and they had seen an explosion of opportunity. During those three summer months in Vegas, Aaron and Sandra took with them one hundred thousand dollars to gamble. These were obviously high stakes, and because of this, the Rocklins were personally called by their last name from the moment they got into

town, to the moment they were dropped off at the

airport. On this particular trip, it was not just about

gambling, but to explore a business opportunity. The

offer in '55 was to be part owners in a new casino,

though that was not their passion, it was just the means.

The Rocklins had several highly successful jewelry stores

in West Virginia.

After the war ended, Aaron left the Army as a

Colonel and him and Sandra settled in New York for a

brief time before relocating to West Virginia. During his

time in the war, Aaron spent most of his active duty in

Germany where, through various channels, got to know

several gemologists who were academically trained in

gemology. One of these trained gemologists took Aaron

to Antwerp to see firsthand the diamond trade, and to

introduce him to other diamond and precious stone

experts. Aaron and Sandra made several trips back to Antwerp, and decided to go into the jewelry business. West Virginia was an opportunity just waiting to happen. Retail and commercial stores were cheap, and it was a great place to raise a family. They started with one rather small store, but concentrated on high end diamonds, sapphires and watches. By the time they opened their second store, they had secured a professionally trained jeweler who made custom pieces for Marilyn Monroe, Elizabeth Taylor, Elvis Presley, James Dean and Frank Sinatra. It was actually Frank Sinatra who made the first introduction to Meyer Lansky, Frank Costello and Bugsy Siegel, just two months before he was killed. It was Frank who persuaded Aaron to visit Las Vegas as a business opportunity.

In 1956, after years of planning, a meeting with

most of the owners of the eight casinos took place where

Aaron's legacy began to form. If Aaron and Sandra were

going to move to Las Vegas, they wanted to have a

vested interest in one of the casinos and be able to

operate their jewelry store. They were given a 10%

ownership in the Tropicana, which was set to open in

1957. Frank Costello, a silent investor, and J. Kell

Housells agreed to the 10%, as long as the first jewelry

store was put inside the Tropicana. During Aaron's

meeting the day before, seven of the owners were

present, and could not agree on where the other stores

would be located. It was ultimately agreed upon that

based on seniority of when the casino opened, they

would have first right of refusal. It ended up being the

Sahara and the Desert Inn as the other casinos to offer

the inhouse jewelry stores, with two others to be opened

somewhere on the Las Vegas Strip. This was a good

compromise between the families, and everyone would share in the profits, without having to hurt anyone.

The idea was that once people won money at the tables and machines; they would have to walk past the jewelry stores. Odds were that if a lady was present, they would be walking in with their winnings and walking out with gold and jewels. Aaron and Sandra would make 60%, and give 40% back to the house. Vegas was all about what you drove, where you lived, and what accessories you were wearing. Everyone loved to impress with jewelry, men and women alike. What better way to celebrate your gambling win than with a new ring, necklace, or Rolex watch? Jewelry stores were nothing new in 1956, but having an established clientele and a name that people knew, it was a win-win for all parties. With jewelry sales, the profits were two to three times the wholesale price of jewelry. Jewelry stores were always willing to negotiate, yet you would never see the

price drop more than half. Never pay the asking price,

but always expect to pay a premium.

In 1955, the "offer" was too good to turn down.

A little unknown secret, the "offer" to open stores inside

the casinos, was more of a demand, an offer you could

not refuse. The plan was to begin operations in 1956.

During those summer trips to Vegas, Sandra fell in love

with the game of craps. During the summer of 55',

everything went incredibly wrong. Actually, everything

went incredibly wrong over a three-day, long weekend

in May. This is what led to the "offer" the Rocklin's

could not refuse.

Friday, May 27th – Memorial Day weekend

Aaron and Sandra arrived late to Vegas in the

summer of 55'. In the previous years, they have arrived

at the beginning of May, and would leave the first week in August. As their plane touched down at the airport, Sandra was hell-bent on heading straight to their hotel room, jumping in a shower, and bolting to the craps table. She needed to get her fix. Aaron was too tired to make the casino, so Sandra was going solo this particular evening. Unable to secure cash, Sandra used her line of credit: $50,000. In the previous six years, 18 months of playing on the casino floor she'd never needed more than $50,000. Playing and learning the art of craps several years prior, Sandra was no stranger to the odds and payouts of the greatest odds game in the casino. Starting small, she left the field alone for the first five shooters. After 45 minutes, she had amassed a nice little profit, somewhere in the neighborhood of 75k. When it was her turn to take the dice, she went all in. After the point was established, four, she started betting big.

Playing the field, Sandra was on her tenth roll of the dice and had over 150k out on the table. Not feeling the pressure and riding the wave, she continued to roll. By this time, there was a rather large gathering around the table. Needing a four, and knowing the odds, Sandra put her remaining 50k on the double two's. Looking down at her chips, she was clean, completely out of her original chips, and all profits up to this point, everything was out on the table.

Her eyes were fixated on the middle of the table, the field. With one hand, picking up the two dice, she raised them to her mouth and gave them a good luck kiss. With a fling of the wrist, the dice were in the air, hitting the table and ricocheting back onto the playing field. Watching with anticipation, the dice tumbled over and over until finally hitting its resting numbers, double two's! With the roar of the crowd, the pit boss began paying out the winnings. Sandra just made $600,000, on top of her original line of credit. $350k alone came from the bet on double twos. Seven-to-one odds are not bad for a 50-thousand-dollar bet. She was still the shooter.

The table that began with seven players was now full of a standing gallery of spectators, and extra security was called in to ensure the safety of the players. Sandra selected her two dice from the lot, and threw them down to establish a new point. Four came up again. She smiled.

Rather than starting slow this time and building up to the field, seeing how the dice would treat her, Sandra had other plans. Looking at the dice on the table that were pushed her way by the stickman, she glanced at her chips. With a slight grin on her face, and listening to the little voice in her head, she began throwing chips out on the table. Within three minutes, she glanced down again, and every single chip was locked and loaded, on the table. By this time, there were no other games in progress; they were all glued on this table.

Sandra gave the Boxman a wink and collected her dice. This had the makings of a heavyweight title fight. Hordes of people, twenty deep, yelling and cheering. Security was now strategically lining the table, roping off a separation of players and spectators. People were running over just to get a glimpse of all the excitement. Nothing attracts a crowd, like a crowd. Even the band on the lounge stage stopped playing, and stood watching through a thick haze of smoke, from their vantage point on the elevated stage. With another kiss of the dice, she let them fly. Sandra's heart rate was slightly elevated, but she was calm. The first dice came to rest in the middle of the table, a "two". The second bounced off another player's chips, and jumped straight into the air, hitting the top of the table and landing on the shoe of the person standing across from her. One of the dealers looked under the table and saw the lone die. He briefly looked at the Boxman, who gave him a nod. The dealer bent down to grab the die and handed it directly to the Boxman. He took the die, surveyed it, and replaced it in the grouping of the other five. The Stickman pushed the collection toward Sandra. Staring intently at the group, Sandra reached down to pick up one of the dice. Raising it up to her lips, she gave it her signature kiss and threw it across the table. At that moment, time stood still. The room was silent. You could hear the old lady sitting at the end of the bar taking a drag off her half-lit cigarette and exhaling the smoke. As the die flew through the air it came crashing down onto the table. With the first bounce, the crowd let out a gasp, waiting with anticipation as it came to a rest.

With a heavy blink and a turn of the head to follow the landing, the Boxman, sitting at the center of the table smiled. Another "two" appeared. The silence was no longer. The dealer once again looked at the Boxman, who looked up at the pit manager who was standing over the table. The manger gave the nod to the Boxman, who returned the nod to the dealer.   The crowd erupted with excitement. It was the shot heard around the world. The Boxman had to stand up and call to the manager to request more chips. It was a massive payout. The time was now three in the morning and Sandra had just eclipsed three million dollars in chips. She was done for the evening. She looked at the pit manger, casino manager and Boxman, and gave them a smile.

"We will take care of that for you Ms. Rocklin," said the casino manager.

"Give each of yourselves one thousand each, thank you."

Sandra called out as she turned away from the table.

Sandra retired for the evening and went to share her

news with Aaron, who had been asleep for almost five

hours already. She would have to wait until morning.

Saturday, May 28th

Saturday was going to be a busy but hopefully a

productive day for the Rocklin's. This was the day

Aaron and Sandra were going to meet the collection of

casino owners to discuss potential business

opportunities. This was one of the only times that you

would get all the casino owners together, in one room, to

discuss something other than eliminating a problem.

This had the potential for everyone to make a lot of

money.

Having barely slept, Sandra was restless as she

was dreaming of her three million dollars. Around 10:30

AM, Sandra kissed Aaron and told him to go ahead

without her. Not in the mood to argue or try to convince

her otherwise, Aaron knew exactly what her plans were.

He kissed her on the cheek and wished her good luck.

Sandra did not wait around for Aaron to leave the hotel

room; she headed back downstairs to the casino floor to

resume where she'd left off the night before. Going to

the cage and signing for her three million dollars' worth

of chips, she headed to the same table. Unfortunately,

the table was not as nice to her as it was a mere few

hours ago. Within two hours, Sandra had lost two

million dollars. Determined to not let this affect her, she

continued to play. Up and down, shooter after shooter,

Sandra had built up her winnings once again to just

under three million. By this time, the table had turned

over ten times, with new players coming and going, but

no one able to keep up with Sandra. It was now six in the evening; Sandra had been playing craps for eight hours straight. Aaron came up from behind and kissed her on the cheek.

"Going well, my dear?"

"Yes, been up and down, but the table is treating me well so far. How was the meeting?"

"Very good. I can fill you in when you come up to the room. We have a few decisions to make before heading home tomorrow. I wish you could have been there, but we have a great thing going here. We may be calling this place home very soon," Aaron replied.

With a smile and a tilt of her head, Sandra kissed Aaron on the lips and said to come get her at the top of the hour so they could eat. He smiled back and went to their penthouse. That was when the luck turned and not in a good way.

Craps is a funny game. Just when you think you have it figured out, it turns on you. For all the time you spend learning the game, playing the game, and betting on the game, it does not care. It will take you for everything you've got, and it will move on to the next player. Craps is a cold-hearted bitch. The night was getting late, and the table was stacked with victims. Sandra was not a player; she was a gambler. The top of the hour had come and gone, and Aaron had fallen asleep on the couch in the room. The time was now eleven in the evening, Sandra was going on twelve hours of standing at the craps table. As she looked down at her chips, she called the pit manager over to talk.

"I'm sorry Mrs. Rocklin, but we can't give you any more chips," the manager said in a reserved, somber, tone.

The table was just about empty by this time, and

Sandra asked to speak to the casino manager. Sonny came down and asked Sandra to sit.

"Listen Sonny, you know me. My husband and I practically helped build this place. You know I'm good for it." Sandra tried to plead.

"Mrs. Rocklin, if there was something I could do, I would. I have been told that tonight is just not your night."
Sandra sat back in the chair, put on a smile, and pulled out the keys to their Rolls Royce.

"Here are the keys to my car. I would like to put this up as collateral. You can't turn that down, can you?"

Sonny got up and walked over to the pit manager. Within five minutes, there were other executives in the huddle discussing the terms.

"Mrs. Rocklin, we can offer you another 100k, but

that is for the car."

Sandra headed back to her spot at the table and picked up the dice. She was the lone person with the dealers. Sonny stayed around to watch. Playing a bit more conservatively, Sandra once again built up a nice pile of chips, but that didn't last long. Within an hour, she was once again pleading with Sonny for more money. It was now two in the morning. Without any more chips and in the middle of her roll, Sandra pulled off her diamond bracelet, her sapphire earrings, and her Vacheron Constantin watch, and placed them in the center of the table. She then picked up the dice and threw them across the table, and rolled a seven.

Sonny walked over to the Boxman and Stickman. The casino chips were covered, and wooden flexible stick was laid to rest on the center of the table. Both walked away. Sonny then picked up the phone and must have only said a few words before hanging up. A few minutes later, two gentlemen appear wearing dark sunglasses, dark suits, and slicked-back hair.

"Mrs. Rocklin, can you please come with us," said one of the gentlemen. They both turned around and started walking. Sandra stood there, looking at Sonny.

"We are not asking, Mrs. Rocklin." Sonny stood behind Sandra and escorted her to the elevator to the second floor. When the doors opened, it was dark. Stepping out, Sandra could see a dim light at the end of the hall, with the door opened halfway. Sandra was escorted into the back office. The two men and Sonny left the room and closed the door behind them. From behind a large oak desk, a monotone, deep voice slowly spoke.

"Mrs. Rocklin, we seem to have a problem," the voice behind the desk said.

"It seems that you owe me a lot of money."

"I want to talk to Aaron. Call my husband now!" Sandra said in a slightly shaken voice.

"No one is calling your husband. You will be lucky to see your husband again, Mrs. Rocklin."

"And what the fuck does that mean?" Sandra said, reluctantly.

"Well, since you asked, I am going to have those two fellas who brought you here, walk right up those stairs and cut the head off that fucking husband of yours. Then, they are going to bring that head into my office and place it right here," pointing to the corner of the desk.

"Any more questions?"
The room was silent.

"Good. Now, as I was saying. It seems that you owe me a lot of money. I have no more interest in your cars or jewelry. I don't want your house. I don't want

your husband. Do you know what I want?"

After a long pause, "No Sir, I do not know what

you want."

"Mrs. Rocklin, what I want are your jewelry

stores. I want your stores in Virginia, and I want your

stores here."

"It's West Virginia," Sandra said

"Mrs. Rocklin, what I want are your jewelry

stores in WEST Virginia."

Sunday, May 29th – 5:30 AM

"Good morning my dear," Aaron said to his wife

as he was making his way to the kitchen.

Sandra was sitting at the kitchen table, wearing the same

clothes as the night before.

"We need to talk," she said.

Aaron stopped Sandra after 30 minutes. Staring out of the penthouse window, shaking his head, Aaron walked over to the phone. Sandra sat quietly, listening to the conversation.

Aaron hung up the phone.

"You are in the clear. You can no longer play in this casino. And the store that we open up here, in this casino, will not be owned by us. We will manage the store, but we will see no revenue from it. This is the best we could have hoped for. You need to thank Frank Costello for allowing us to walk away tonight. Now let's go."

****

Frankie and Charlie grew up in and around the operations of the jewelry store. Their parents wanted them to learn the family business and hoped for the

eventual passing of the proverbial torch. But if you had

asked Frankie or Charlie, that was the last thing they

wanted to do with their lives, although it was always

interesting. Who knew that being in the jewelry business

was a chance to meet top entertainers, showroom

dancers, actors, singers, and even an occasional hitman?

As they grew older, job offers were plentiful because of

who their parents were, but Frankie and Charlie never

took advantage of that. There were distinct advantages

to knowing the right people in Vegas; front row tickets

to the heavyweight fights, going backstage to meet

Sammy Davis Jr., or greeting Evel Knievel before his

attempt to jump the famed fountains at Caesars Palace.

After high school graduation, however, Frankie and

Charlie went off to college instead of staying home to

take over the stores. It was a nice lifestyle, but they

wanted to do their own thing, rather than just be known

as the "Rocklin and Rotchedo kids."

****

As Charlie drove up to the restaurant to pick up

his food, the valet knew to keep his car nearby. Charlie

ran inside to get his soup and sandwich and was back in

the car to go home where he would eat in solitude on his

deck overlooking Lake Tahoe. Saturdays were always

spent like this: a few hours in the morning at the office

and lunch out on the deck. Saturday was the day to hit

"Refresh" before the Sunday gorilla. Outside of the

office visit, Charlie rarely left his house on Saturdays.

Unless it was raining or snowing, you would find him

basking in the sun. He did not turn on his computer or

read the paper; he just sat there, often watching the

sunset and enjoying an old fashioned. Charlie kept

notebooks around the house in which he wrote notes,

ideas and other random thoughts that crossed his mind.

Knowing that his work week started on Sunday

morning, this was how he regenerated for the upcoming

week. Since his first day working as a licensed broker,

Saturdays had always been reserved for rest. It was so

important to have a day to refresh, refocus, and take a

step back. This was one piece of advice he shared with

his clients; one message he delivered with every

speaking engagement, and one something that he

himself never deviated from. It didn't have to be

Saturday; it just had to be one day a week where you did

nothing related to your job.

After eating his lunch, Charlie stretched out on

the futon on the deck, and fell asleep under the Tahoe

sun.

Chapter Three

"Good morning Mr. Rocklin. Welcome back from Chicago. Hope your weekend went well and hope you got some rest, because you're going to need it. I'll be in to review last week and go over your calendar for this week," said Doris, Charlie's personal secretary.

Charlie unlocked the door to his office and walked toward his desk. Before he even took his coat off, the phone began to ring. Three people were in the lobby waiting to talk to him. Doris made her way past them, a tablet under her arm and a handful of messages. Just as Doris began to speak, Charlie looked at the others who promptly turned around and walked back out of the office.

"David Duffield will be here at nine o'clock to drop off a

check. He wanted to personally drop it off, and set up a

follow up meeting on a new venture he's looking at.

Your ten is Stephen Clay, he just became the CEO of

Yahoo and wants to meet regarding a restructure idea

for Sunnyvale. If you want Vestberg to give his

approval, we can set up a meeting. Clay was referred by

Buffett. Then you're off to present your portfolio to Old

Greenwood and their invited guests for consideration of

a new clubhouse in preparation of the PGA tour event

they'll be hosting in August. You will be having lunch

with David Coverdale at the club at 12:15. At 1:00, you

have a conference call with Ken Miyauchi from Softbank

in Tokyo, which you can take on your cell. It's very early

for them, but that is the only time you had available this

week. I will call you at 12:55 to set it up. Ken has a

question about a line item in your report. It should be no

longer than fifteen minutes. You also have a note in

Outlook to call Frankie regarding tonight. I put that in your calendar as a task at 1:30. Once you get back to the office, you have about an hour to return calls before you're off to Montana to meet with John Hyde, the President of Shell Oil. You should take off from here no later than 2:30 to be there at 4:30 and meet at 5:00. I will have a car waiting. If you'd like to stay the night, let me know; otherwise, I'll have the Ruben stay on board so you can be home by 10:00 p.m. And don't forget to drop off the Maserati for oil and tire rotation so it will be ready in the morning." You would think that someone with that much money would have someone else drop off the Maserati, but no one drove Charlie's cars but Charlie.

This was a typical day for Charlie. When he was actually in town and in the office, Doris had the same routine. Even when he is traveling, Doris syncs up with

Charlie by Teams every morning to review the day.

Charlie is often away from his office, so he

communicates by using Microsoft Teams and if he needs

anything for a meeting or a client, he has the office

runner hand deliver the items to him, no matter where

he is. Most of his files are on the cloud, and everything

Doris says in the morning huddles, are organized in

OneNote, so Charlie can access at any time. Although

most files are available electronically, there are some

situations, where Charlie likes to have the paper file in

his hand. Last month while in Atlanta meeting with a

client, Charlie needed a file that was at the office.

Instead of having Federal Express or UPS deliver the file

overnight, he sent for the runner, who delivered it

personally within five hours. Not only does it ensure

that the file will get to Charlie as quickly as physically

possible, it impresses the clientele immensely. "Image is

everything." And having your own private plane is nice, too. Charlie has two planes, in case there was a need for emergency travel, such as a missing file, for instance.

It was now 12:00 p.m., and Charlie was at the Club waiting for Coverdale to arrive. And it is always interesting having a meal with David Coverdale. You never know if he will show up alone, or with women on each arm. The last time Charlie had lunch with this man, it lasted 10 minutes, David's phone was blowing up from several women he met the night before. On his way back to the car to retrieve a file, Charlie noticed a Bentley parked next to him and it was rocking back and forth. As Charlie opened his car door, he heard his name being called. When he turned around, he saw the back window of the Bentley roll down and David poked out his head followed by a plume of smoke and women's laughter. Lunch with David would be slightly delayed.

****

Now seated, Charlie returned a few calls and

checked his email. The waiter brought him an iced tea;

that was when he noticed a woman. He noticed her

walk by and saw her look in his direction. Completely

oblivious to the conversation on the other end of the

phone, Charlie hung up in mid-sentence and sent the

interrupted call directly to voice mail when his phone

rang again.

She was wearing white golf pants with a sapphire

blue, collared polo shirt. As she took off her sunglasses

and turned her head toward Charlie, she smiled. She

tilted her head and presented her ultra-white teeth. No

words were spoken, not even a seductive lip-sync hello

or a slight wave; just a simple and seemingly innocent

smile. Charlie could not turn his head. He tried, but his eyes were glued to this woman. Sure, he had seen beautiful women before, but not like this. *Who was she?* Suddenly, there was no one else in the restaurant. It was Charlie and this amazingly beautiful woman, looking back at him. She had fabulous long brown hair that curled at the ends and bounced with every step as she went to her table and took a seat. Her smile was as breathtaking as her overall appearance. He had to meet her - there was no other option.

He noted where she was sitting and got up to introduce himself. He approached her table. Charlie never got nervous, but today, he was nervous. He was beginning to perspire and could feel it on his upper lip. He wiped the palm of his hands with the napkin from the table.

"Hi, I'm Charlie Rocklin," he said in his most

confident voice.

"Hello, Charlie Rocklin" she replied, seemingly with no emotion. After a brief moment of silence, she gave him a half-smile.

"My name is Serina. Have you eaten lunch already, or would you care to join me?"

"Actually, I would love to, but I'm here for a business meeting and then off to meet a client. But how about lunch tomorrow?", he replied.

"That would be nice. How about if we meet here at 11:30 a.m." Serina proposed.

With a smile and a nod, Charlie accepted Serina's offer. He turned away, still grinning, and strolled back to join David, who was now waiting at the table.

Not knowing what the hell had just happened, Charlie felt rocked, his foundation shaken. Lunch was difficult that day. When meeting with anyone, be a

client or a friend, there was no one more important than
the person he was talking to, no distractions with his full
attention. With the amount of money he commanded,
there should never be a distraction. But something had
overcome Charlie. He was confused. David was sitting
directly in front of him, talking and moving his hands,
going on and on about how he wants to sell his home of
30 years and what to do with the money. A fifth-glass-
of-scotch vocabulary was coming from David's mouth,
but in Charlie's mind, it was just background noise. He
could taste the smell of scotch coming from the other
side of the table, but he took in no words. Trying to keep
his focus and maintain eye contact with David, he
couldn't help but keep turning his head to get a glance of
the woman who had literally taken his breath away.
Serina got up from her table, took her last sip of water
with lemon, and walked out, but not before she gave

Charlie one more flash of that smile. She left with a

satisfied expression on her face.

Charlie went to bed restless that night. Every

time he closed his eyes, visions of Serina danced around.

He could not wait for sunrise. He was unable to

concentrate on anything that night or the next morning.

He went to the club early and reserved the entire

restaurant. For all existing reservations, he offered each

table a $1,000, as an apology. Charlie sat impatiently and

watched the time. 11:30 came and went and he was still

seated alone at his table, alone in the restaurant. It was

now 12:05. Serina never made it to lunch that day.

Charlie had no idea if she'd been in an accident, or had

just decided not to show up, and his mind toggled both

possibilities. He did not have her number; he did not

know her last name. He asked everyone at the

restaurant who she was, and if they remembered her

from the day before, but no one did. This was a dead end. Charlie was in unchartered territory; he was not accustomed to being stood up, and he'd never been in a position where he did not have the power.

The next two months crawled by as if life was moving in slow motion. Meetings came and went, planes took off and landed, but the days were a blur. Charlie was physically present, but not really there. Although the introduction was brief, he could not get the mysterious Serina off his mind. After two months of replaying what he could have done differently, if it was something he said, or didn't say, he had no other option but to let it go. Some things in life are just not meant to be, and some are just irrational. Was this a deeper message that there was something missing in his life? Was someone trying to tell Charlie that he needed to look beyond his current plan and search for something or someone else? Fuck it. It was all an illusion. Charlie

needed to get grounded and refocused. There was only

one person who really knew the answer, and that was

Serina and she was gone.

****

On June 11th, at 11:30 a.m., Charlie was waiting

on a lunch meeting at the Windsor Steak House on the

North Shore of Lake Tahoe. On a day with the crystal,

glistening sun shining down, Charlie was outside under

the canopy talking to Doris on the phone. The topic of

the day was his upcoming trip to Japan to meet and

consult with the CEO of Mazda Corporation, specifically

dealing with importing cars to North America. Mazda

was doing fine in their native land, but their sales had

been dropping in the States for the past ten years. They

had not had a new and exciting launch since the Miata and had discontinued the once-famed RX-7. Reliance on one model, was no longer returning the dividends projected. Today it is no longer manufactured, nor would it sell due to its lack of long-term reliability. Charlie's forte was not designing new automobiles, or advising on manufacturing, but understanding the supply and demand that resulted in the bottom line. Mazda had tried to focus their market on the older generation but could not compete with American makers like Cadillac and Buick. What was the best way to minimize cost, reduce redundancy, and maximize output, resulting in increased profit? Is it cost, quality or service? Can any of those be solved with people, processes or systems? That is exactly what Charlie will determine.

Not all companies who call Charlie are in dire

straits. Some are just looking for an outside perspective,

a comparative analysis of their competition, or simply a

review of their current positions and financials. Charlie

takes every referral call and talks to the prospective

client before making his decision whether to work with

them or wish them success with someone else. The

constant calls, meetings, and long trips were occasionally

a nuisance, but a good problem to have for a company

just over 9 years old.

"Please arrive at the hanger at 7:00 in the

morning tomorrow. You will be going into DFW before

headed into Tokyo, and then Osaka. Mazda will have a

car waiting for you. Do you want to stay over a few

days, or turn around and come back?" Doris sat quietly

on the other end, awaiting a response.

"Charlie? You there?" Doris said inquisitively.

With the phone to his ear, Charlie suddenly saw

Serina appear before him. He had just reached for his tablet to confirm his trip details when he noticed the sun being blocked by a shadowy figure. He looked up; it was her. Charlie's grin quickly turned to a big smile of delight. It was as if it was early Christmas morning, and he had just found Santa climbing up the chimney.

"Charlie? Can you hear me?" Doris asked again.

Charlie abruptly hung up the phone. Serina stood there before him, with the rays of sun wrapping her figure like a distant mirage. She was wearing a red dress with white lace trim. Her hat was large enough to cover two heads and blocked the sun from her eyes. Charlie nearly leapt out of his chair.

"Please join me?" Charlie asked.

Without speaking a word, Serina nodded, and sat down across from him. Sitting back down and gazing into her eyes for a moment, Charlie finally spoke.

"What happened to you? You didn't show up at Old Greenway." Before she could even answer, he continued.

"Are you alright? I don't even know you, but you had me worried. Actually, I've not even been able to focus. You have been my distraction. I can't believe you're here, now."

Serina reached out and touched Charlie's arm as if to calm a distraught child.

"I'm so sorry. Something came up, and I wasn't able to make it," she replied. "I would have called, but I didn't know how to reach you. I don't even know your last name. I called the Club, but they said you hadn't arrived. I didn't mean to worry you Charlie."

"So, you're here now, why don't we go get some lunch?" he asked.

"Aren't you meeting someone for lunch? What

about your meeting Charlie?" Serina said.

"Yes, well, I can have the meeting some other time. I can just make a call and reschedule for later in the day. Will that work for you? It will just take a moment."

"No, not today. I saw your car outside and decided to stop and say 'hello'. I'm on my way to meet some friends who are staying at Harrah's. I'll call you later. She got up from the table and started to walk away before he could reply.

Charlie, watched in silence as Serina walked away, "but aren't you forgetting something he said." Staring at the back of her dress as she turned around, "and what am I forgetting Charlie?"

"My number, you don't have my number."

"I know how to find you." And she left the room.

Charlie felt a slight sense of déjà vu. It was the dress and the obscenely large hat. The elevator in his building, that is where he saw Serina, chills shot through Charlie's body. Charlie got up from the table and went to find Serina. As he made his way through the dining room, Charlie's client showed up and started talking, interrupting his train of thought.

"Charlie, how the hell are you? Long time brother. What have you been up to, besides making a shitload of money?"

Charlie was still dazed and gazing off into the distance. Before he could fully process what just happened, Serina was gone.

With the walk of a defeated heavyweight, Charlie turned around and he and Ben walked to his table. He found it very hard to concentrate on the business at hand, but he managed. Fortunately, this was not his first meeting with Ben; this was a follow-up meeting, and Charlie was going to collect a retainer check in the amount of two million dollars.

Charlie didn't understand why people are still writing checks instead of wiring money, but some of his clients still preferred face to face and writing checks. It was a lost artform, but Charlie respected that, considering the amount of money he commanded, he happily met with small minority of those embracing the writing of checks. He had already provided a report to the board and given them some preliminary papers, leading up to the increased fee that he was requiring. Ben continued to carry on a one-sided conversation, and every so often Charlie smiled and nodded. His mind, however, was exploding. Staring off into space, Charlie's eyes squinted as he began to play out scenarios in his head.

He asked himself, *how did Serina know what kind of car I drive? And that dress and hat, why would she wear that same outfit again? Was she trying to tell me something that she couldn't in the elevator?* Charlie did not miss too many details, but this had him spinning.

Charlie returned to the office to retrieve messages and return a few calls. One of the messages was from a longtime family friend, Ray Regionareo. Ray had been a good friend of Charlie's parents and had known Charlie since he was a little boy. Ray now lived in Florida most of the time and had a house in Vegas, as well, but rarely visited. He was a retired FBI agent, turned undercover informant, so he knew a lot of people from all walks of life. He had helped Charlie's parents out of a few jams, and they had rewarded him rather handsomely. After he retired from service, Aaron made Ray the collector for the stores. His primary job was to track down customers who did not pay or find out something that was not so easy to find out. Often, people would purchase jewelry by paying installments. Once half the balance had been paid, the customer was entitled to take possession of the jewelry. If a payment was missed, the Rocklin's would call Ray. Ray's job was simply to get the payment. If payment was not immediately made, then he would repossess the product, using whatever method he deemed necessary. In return, Charlie's parents made sure he was taken care of for the rest of his life. Ray always promised the Rocklin's that if anything ever happened to them, he would watch out for Charlie.

"Ray, Charlie here. How are things in Florida?"

"Not too bad buddy, not bad at all. Man, you gotta come down here, it's a wonderful place to be. The weather is heaven, and the girls are everywhere. If I didn't know any better, I'd say they were falling off the trees. And boy, do they eat their veggies. These girls are in good shape. Very healthy, Charlie. Makes me cry at night, knowing I'm just getting older and they're getting younger!"

"I have a feeling that you didn't call me to discuss the abundance of women in Florida," Charlie said with a slight grin. Even though they hadn't talked in a few months, Charlie was in no mood to make small talk.

"No, no, I didn't call to talk to you about Florida or the women here. I will be in town on Thursday to tie up a few things, and I need to talk to you."

"Is everything alright? Are you in some kind of trouble?" Charlie asked.

"No, not really. I just need to talk to you, in person and in private. This is important, do you hear me?"

"Yeah, I hear you. But you have me somewhat concerned. Are you sure you're, okay?"

"I'm sorry to say, but this trip is not about me; it is about you, my friend. We need to talk. So, you will pick me up at the airport on Thursday? My flight lands in Tahoe at 1:00 a.m., the redeye."

"Yes. Sure, I'll be there. I can pick you up; I highly doubt I have anything on my calendar at that time. And why the hell are you taking the redeye? I can send the jet for you. I guess retirement isn't as good as you thought it would be?" Charlie said, trying to make light of the conversation.

"Fuck you, Charlie. No, I'm good, I can take a regular plane just like everyone else on this planet other than you. And please do not talk to anyone strange. Oh, and you need to bring Beauty. I love that fucking car."

"Sure thing, Ray. See you Thursday."

"One more thing, Charlie. Can I drive?"

"I'll see you on Thursday," Charlie chuckled.

"Actually, I'll see you Friday, early!"

A rather strange call, but Ray was a straightforward, no bullshit kind of guy. If something is on his mind, he will usually tell you straight up, and won't give a damn who it is about or who it will affect. An admirable characteristic, but it can be brutally honest. Ray was a guy you always wanted in your corner. He would take a bullet for you, and still carry you out on his back.

Tuesday came quickly for Charlie. He had stayed up late on conference calls with clients in China and Singapore. Charlie often liked to monitor the companies for which he consulted, to observe his progress. He kept a running progress report on himself, a matrixed scorecard, to chart his successes and areas in need of improvement. If the companies' results were less than expected, he would perform portfolio reviews at no charge and provide detailed reports back to his clients. Most of the time, he presented back to the client before they even knew there was a problem. This was not the norm; Charlie very rarely had to do anything free of charge, but on the rare occasion when there was a missing variable that he could not control, he would make it right. Every call he made was documented, and every transaction was written down in the portfolio. He recorded the date and time of each call, to whom he talked, for how long, and exactly what they discussed; business or not, it was written down.

At 5:30 a.m., his phone rang. It was Doris calling to remind Charlie of his meeting with Michael Manns. Michael Manns was a guy who was at the right place at the right time in the early Eighties. During his college days, to help pay for books and beer, Michael delivered

latex gloves to local hospitals and clinics. Within a year,

he had contracts with most of the major hospitals and

doctor offices along the entire East coast. He was able to

purchase large quantities of gloves and undercut the

usual reps who supplied to the same places. His profit

margins were not huge and in fact, he lost money on

some deals just to get the contract. Not only was he

delivering gloves, he became the main East coast

distributor. He was able to maintain his studies while

delivering the gloves on the days he did not have class.

With the contacts he established and services he

provided; his business soon became the number one

latex glove distributor in the country. He received

favorable pricing and passed this along to his clients,

continuing to edge out the competition. For other major

medical suppliers, dealing with latex gloves was pennies

compared to the other services or equipment they

provided, so Michael seldom ran up against any real

competition. College soon dropped to a second priority

on his list, while he focused on gloves.

Then in mid-1981, the AIDS epidemic publicly

surfaced. There were cases prior to the 80's, but there

was not enough sophisticated evidence or testing to

identify what the true cause of illness or even death.

After several patients died in the late 1970's and into 81,

a journalist wrote about this "strange" disease that was

killing people. Then in July of 81, the *New York Times* ran

a similar article, and the world was now taking notice of

something that had previously been kept in secret.

Although the term "AIDS" was not officially coined until

1982, Michael was suddenly inundated with orders for

massive quantities of latex gloves. Doctors' offices,

hospitals, clinics, private homes, schools, businesses, and

government offices all were placing orders. His

company, Biocentric, appeared in magazines,

newspapers, and documentaries. Biocentric was getting

acquisition offers from companies all over the world. A

bidding war ensued, and soon the offers were too good

to ignore. One particular offer included not only a great

deal of cash, north of $100 million, but also included

part-ownership in the parent company and a position as

Vice President, overseeing international shipping and

procurement of product. Michael ultimately sold his

college company for $125 million dollars and a

significant number of stock options, and became Vice

President of operations for Kimberly Clark, Inc. He was

25.

Michael approached Charlie with the idea to

expand Kimberly Clark into under-developed countries

to promote sanitation and help stimulate the countries'

economies, while achieving great visibility for the

company, but with the goal of stopping the spread of

diseases. Kimberly Clark already made the gloves that

Michael sold, but they did not have his contacts or

contracts with the hospitals, clinics, medical offices,

schools, or county and state offices. They also had a

solid grasp on medical supplies in the United States but

did very little philanthropy. Michael wanted to change

this, and even donated some of this annual salary to

offset the cost of shipping supplies to these countries.

When Michael approached Charlie, it really had nothing

to do with making money, but how to make the most of

his money while donating some to a great cause. Charlie

took the meeting with nothing more in mind other than

hear what Michael had to say. Clean water and

sanitation in small third-world countries was a luxury

that did not exist. Michael was determined to put his

money to work for someone other than himself. Even if
the efforts where small, such as donating latex gloves,
the impact could save lives. Michael was looking to
Charlie to help formulate a business plan he could
present to the Kimberly Clark Board of Directors.
Michael was headed for Australia and decided to meet
with Charlie while his plane re-fueled at the Lake Tahoe
airport. Normally, Charlie had a higher standard for a
meeting place, but under the circumstances, he met
Michael at the airport.

Their meeting lasted three hours. As Michael
boarded his plane, Charlie watched. They were now
partners in this endeavor. Michael had a viable idea, but
not for a company like Kimberly Clark. They had plans
to start a foundation, just the two of them, and then they
could approach companies, including Kimberly Clark,
and other medical and pharmaceutical companies to

donate to their cause. Why be limited to the resources of just one company when you can broaden your reach and have a greater impact for those who need it most? Eliminate Foundation was about to become a global leader in helping cure and stop the spread of diseases. *Eliminate the cause, eliminate the need to worry.*

Charlie and Michael went on to be not only partners in the foundation, but also close friends. They both had larger aspirations with their money and wanted to create something new, something that others would also have a passion for. With their own money and wealthy friends and clients, Eliminate Foundation would become one of the largest privately funded non-profit foundations in the world.

At 9:30 in the evening, everyone else had gone home. His eyes red from staring at his computer all afternoon. Charlie closed his laptop and decided to head home for the night. He walked around turning off the office lights, and then went back to lock his office door. The office grew dark, with only the shadow of nearby buildings reflected off the walls from the light of the moon. As he picked up his coat that was lying on the back of the sofa, the private phone line in his office rang, startling Charlie. Charlie has many international clients, so it was not unusual to get calls late into the night, but on his private line, that was peculiar. The ringing stopped. Charlie took his coat and headed for the door. Closing the door behind him, the phone began to ring again, Charlie went back in to answer.

"This is Charlie."

On the other end was a faint voice he could barely hear, but what he did hear gave him chills.

"I can see you right now."

"Did you say you can see me right now? You

need to speak up, I cannot hear you. Who is this?"

Charlie asked as the chill ran up and down his whole

body.

"I am watching you, Charlie. You will not get

away."

Holding the phone to his ear, Charlie looked

around the office and walked to the drawn blinds on his

window. Peeking out with one finger, he saw an empty,

dark parking lot.

"Are you done?" he asked

There was silence on the other end, but he could

hear the faint sounds of someone breathing as he hung

up. From behind his desk, he could see the long, dark

hallway outside his office door. Charlie took a deep

breath and grabbed the inside of his jacket. Inside,

holstered, was a Smith and Wesson .357 Magnum,

loaded with hollow points. As he gripped the handle, he

walked through his office door and closed it tight behind him. Walking down the moonlit hallway into the lobby, he signaled for the elevator. Heading to his car in the garage, he continued to look around. Chills returned as he made his approach to the driver's door, knowing this was not the first time he'd had a strange encounter in this garage. Even as he drove home, he looked at every passing car, keenly aware of his surroundings. Yet nothing seemed out of the ordinary, other than that fucking freaky fucker who called.

Wednesday. 5:03 a.m.

"Charlie, rise and shine. This is a reminder that you're scheduled to have a telephone conference at 7:30 here at the office, and the Dillon Investment Group is coming in to talk to you at 8:00," phoned Doris. "Would you like me to send a car for you, or do you want to drive today?" she asked.

"No, I'll drive. Thanks. See you in an hour."

Charlie sat up in bed and turned-on CNBC. Brian knocked and opened the bedroom door, carrying a laptop that was already logged into Bloomberg, along with a rolled-up copy of the *Wall Street Journal*, and a glass of freshly squeezed orange juice. Brian had been working for Charlie for four years. He was to Charlie as Alfred was to Batman. Before his wife passed away, Brian worked for Warren Buffet for 20 years. After that, he could not continue living in Omaha, doing the same thing every day; it only reminded him of what he had lost. During a lunch with Charlie, Warren recommended Brian. Within a month, Charlie had all of Brian's belongings sent up to Tahoe and had secured a private area of the house for him.

After a few minutes of Bloomberg and a review

of his appointments for the day, Brian knocked on his door again.

"There's a lady on the line for you. Do you want to take it?"

"Who is it, Brian?"

"She wouldn't give her name, but she said it was urgent."

Puzzled, Charlie decided to take the call. "Sure, I'll pick it up in here, thanks."

Charlie received thousands of calls, but not too often on his home landline.

"Hello, this is Charlie." There was no response from the other end.

"Hello," and again no response. Charlie heard the person hang up.

Putting on a robe, he opened the door to speak to Brian.

"Do you have any idea who that was? She said it was urgent?"

"No, but she asked for you by name, and said she had to speak with you right away. She didn't say anything else."

Not that Charlie was paranoid, but he was beginning to feel a little uneasy. This was the second time in less than two days that someone had called, as if to verify his whereabouts. First it was his private office line and now his home. Both numbers were unpublished, and very few people had those numbers. Charlie packed his gun before leaving the house.

Charlie decided to take the Lotus to the office. Of all the cars Charlie owned, he drove the Lotus most often. It was a Jim Clark edition, of which only 500 were produced by special order. Charlie had ordered his directly from Lotus International. By far not the most exotic of his collection, but very reliable, a rarity among these cars.

Charlie got to work at just after 6:30 in the morning to do a review before his phone conference, and to read up on the investment group coming in at 8:00. About once a month, he would entertain an investment group's pitch. He did not make any promises or guarantees, but he listened. He did this mostly for the benefit of the investment group, to give them the confidence to approach other executives with their ideas. He never went as far as investing in the idea, but thanked them for coming with an "I'll be in touch". Often, he listened to their presentations, giving them feedback on what they did well and what they might want to change. Charlie had entertained over 30 presentations in the past several years and had yet to invest in any of them; but sometimes for the investors, the experience itself far outweighed the actual selling.

Time spent with Charlie to hear *his* ideas and comments,

was what they really came for. Getting an hour with

someone like Charlie was like a politician getting 15

minutes with the President.

Wednesday. 7:30 a.m.

"Charlie, Bill is on the phone," Doris said from

the doorway of Charlie's office.

There are three qualities that Charlie expects out

of his clients, and he reciprocates. The first is to

be on time, second is to be open and the third is

to be honest.

"Charlie, thank you so much for taking this. I

know we aren't scheduled to meet for another couple of

months, but I think we need to talk", Bill Barnett said

over the roundtable.

"Bill, no need to thank me. Now what is on your mind?" Charlie replied.

"It has been three months since we have implemented your plan Charlie, and our numbers have mostly remained the same. In fact, they are beginning to trend down. It was our understanding that with the amount we are reinvesting, we should have seen a positive impact to our numbers by now, our bottom line. We, the executive leaders, the board and myself, have all taken a substantial cut for this fiscal year, and honestly, this is not what we had planned for. We've spent a great deal of time and money with you and expected to see some kind of a return and not one that is treading south. No one is noticing, no one is following us, and we are seeing a decrease in traffic. The wave is not big enough to generate the attention."

"When you refer to 'our understanding', who are

you referring to?" Charlie asked.

"Jack Likes, Romie Romin, and Sky Davis are also here."

"Bill, next time you call me on a conference call, let me know who's joining us and what affiliation they have. I don't have the time to discuss details with you and your partners about my plan that we discussed a few months ago. It has only been two months, with ten more to go to see results. At the time I first met with you and the board, TheStreet.com was a non-profit company. And I'm not talking about an intentional non-profit; you were NOT a 501(c). TheStreet.com lost over 15 million dollars in revenue last year. So far this quarter, as you stated, your numbers have remained the same, or maybe have taken a slight downturn. This time last year, you had lost just under four million dollars. Like I tell everyone, I have no guarantees, and I make no promises.

While I'm confident in every proposal I make, I cannot predict a company's future, nor can I predict the way others will respond. I usually do an analysis after the first six months; we have not reached that point. There is no silver bullet, and if you expected a miracle after two months, then you are in the wrong fairy tale, my friend."

Charlie takes a deep breath and clears his throat

"If after six months, you and your partners share these same concerns, we will talk then. I understand your concerns and investment in this company, but success will not happen overnight. As proposed, within the next couple of months, we will take TheStreet.com public, create more revenue, and begin to offer investment services to remain competitive. When this goes public, it will make you and the rest of the board of directors very wealthy. I will make you more money that 99% of the rest of the working world. Your financial backing, commitment and trust in me is much appreciated. While it is not a guarantee, I will make you all very rich. I have the confidence in my abilities to turn your company into something everyone wants to be a part of. Lastly, I would not have taken you on as a client if I did not think we could turn this around. Please don't question my business motives or ethics."

There was a pause on the line, as if who wants to respond first.

"You're right. We're sitting here looking at one another, saying you're right, we are all nodding our heads. We just got out of a board meeting and are feeling a little heat at the moment. We panicked; I am sorry. There is a shitload of money at stake here."

"No need to apologize for your concerns. You had them on your mind, so you came to me. That is why I'm here, and that is why you hired me. If you have anything else on your mind or any other concerns, just

call. And next time, again, don't do a blind conference

call with me. I will see you in a few months. Doris will

set up a day with you and your partners three months

from now.   Bill, please stay on for Doris."

Charlie transferred the call to Doris and hung up

the phone. It was not that Charlie minded being called

with questions or concerns, he hated to be surprised.

Being open and honest with Charlie is the only way to

stay a client. And if that means just announcing who is

on the call, then you better announce who is on the call.

Wednesday. 8:45 a.m.

Doris walked into Charlie's office to inform him

that the investment group was waiting in the lounge.

The conference call went a little longer than anticipated,

but to the group, it did not matter. This was a chance

that few would ever get, even if it was only 15 minutes. Doris was going to call Charlie at 9:00 a.m., for another meeting away from the office. As the group hustled into the conference room, they used their 15 minutes well. Although they were not able to get through the entire presentation, Charlie gave them a few suggestions and told them he would be in contact with them at a later date. Usually, that meant a note from Charlie thanking them for their time.

"Thank you for taking the time to present to me today gentlemen. The reason why you could not get through the presentation is that it was too long, too much information and too many small details. You must know your audience. When doing a pitch to an investor or a group of high-level executives, you must be intentional, you must be deliberate in your message and with what you are wanting. I suggest you start with why you are here. On your first slide, tell your audience what you want, why you want it, and how much you want. If you don't want anything, then you need to say this. If you only have a few minutes to pitch someone, get to the point. Take the guesswork out of it. This is not a fiction novel with a twist ending. That is all just fucking noise. You need to hook them in the first two minutes; otherwise, you'll lose their attention and any possible opportunities. You are going to be talking to very busy people who don't have time to waste on a presentation that isn't well thought out, planned and intentional with why you are there. Thank you again for your time."

Wednesday. 9:00 a.m.

Right on cue, Doris called Charlie to prepare him for his next appointment. Another member of the office staff escorted the Dillan Group out the door. Charlie grabbed his coat, and out the door he went to meet with Robert Parker of Parker Pens, Inc.

Mr. Parker flew in the previous night, having decided to take advantage of Tahoe that evening by relaxing on his balcony. Charlie was on his way to meet with Mr. Parker in his $5,000-a-night suite at Harrah's Tahoe. The suite is entered through a double door into a sunken formal dining room. From the dining room, one can go out to the balcony that overlooks Lake Tahoe and snowcapped mountains. The suite had three bedrooms and four bathrooms, all with double vanities and Jacuzzi tubs. The master bedroom is centered around a circular California King-sized bed that is raised in the middle of the room. From the bed you can control the lights, window blinds, or television, answer the door, or make a hands-free phone call from the built-in electrical console next to the bed. Any potential and current clients of

Charlies received the same treatment. The hotel knew to

send a basket of fresh fruit, a bottle of wine, and a

variety of cheeses.

Charlie rang the suite doorbell and saw that

brunch was waiting on the table, with waiters ready to

serve them as they discussed business. Parker pens have

been around for over 120 years. Their name had stood

the test of time, and anyone who knew pens, knew the

name. Today, with competition increasing and more

demand for sophisticated writing instruments, Parker

wanted to do something to shake up their brand.

Robert Parker is a fourth-generation owner and

has relied on his father's and grandfather's advice for

business ideas and ventures. Looking at profits, Robert

thought a change might be in order due to the 8%

decrease of revenue per year over the past five years.

Parker was once a high demand, high quality pen, one of the few in the market that had surpassed the century mark. When Cross pens began to flood the middle market, Parker decided to compete. This was where their business took a turn. Cross was providing the stiffest competition, but the other smaller companies were also taking away from Parker. Their higher line of pens had decreased slightly, but the middle line had been the reason for the large decreasing trend. Because the name had been synonymous with fashion and cost, people didn't think of Parker pens as being "affordable". The less expensive option was generally thought to be Cross, and they had already established a solid customer base catering to the middle class. Now their high-end market was also seeing decreased sales and revenue due to quality issues and status statements with the likes of Pineider, Visconti, Waterman and Montblanc.

Robert had met Charlie at the door and greeted him with a handshake.

"I trust you received the financials, production numbers and market analysis of each line in production?" Robert asked as they made their way to the table.

Charlie had received the documents and already had some ideas before Robert opened the door.

"Robert, a Parker pen is still known throughout the world as a high-quality, reliable writing instrument. A drastic change might make people question the quality and shy away from purchasing them, especially if you take away from your bread and butter. Think of it as if what would happen to Rolex if they started producing jewelry or even pens. They cannot change fundamentally what they are or ignore what they have done to the watch industry. What I can do is change your advertising angle, focus more on the middle class, and make it as if the pens were more affordable to that target audience. Of course, the high line will remain intact and cater to the wealthy, but we'll increase overall familiarity with Parker pens. And I'm not talking just the United States, I'm talking worldwide. People who can afford the Duofold line will remain loyal to a product they know and trust. Those who are in the market for a new high-quality pen, we need to draw them to Parker or back to Parker".

Robert's posture turned a little more relaxed as if he wanted to hear more.

"We need to introduce, 'Parker' as a household name. Once word spreads that Parker is getting aggressive with market penetration, it will generate attention and interest, as well as more competition. We need to attack Cross and go head-to-head, making them aware that we are still here and relevant in the market. The goal is to make your competition worry and take notice, force them reevaluate their own product lines, their own target audience, shake some shit up. Make them re-think their strategic marketing. Every company needs to 'reinvent' themselves at some point in their history. Becoming complacent is a death sentence. Those on top, don't stay on top, there are always others waiting behind the door to just get a foot in. Revitalizing a stagnant market will cause everyone to get up, take notice, and take a look at what they are doing. In this market, we are not seeing many new entries. We know who the competition is, now we just need to become relevant again."

Charlie notices Robert crossing his arms. This is usually a sign of resistance. Charlie takes a sip of his iced tea and continues.

"I'll need to review your current and past production reports along with expenditures and the last five years of audited financials. I'll also need details of advertising dollars spent over the past ten years. What you sent over was good, but it doesn't give me a complete picture of what Parker has done or where they intend to go. With this information, I can assure you that unproductive actions and repeated failures will be avoided. Once you decide to go with me, we can get into more details about my involvement and cooperation from the members of the board. How did I do?" Charlie sat back in his chair, taking another sip of his iced tea.

"Honestly, this is our first meeting, and you seem to know more about the market and competition than I do! This all sounds fine, but we have increased our advertising dollars within the past year, two-fold in fact. We have invested a great deal of time and money in our current campaign. Making, as you stated, a drastic change that has led us to financial troubles."

"First, please do not underestimate me. When I take a meeting, I come prepared. By our first meeting, I will know as much about your company as you do. By the time you hire me, and I finish my analysis and consolidate that into my presentation and report out, I will know more about your company than you do, that is why people come to me. Second, our meeting is done. If what you have told me is true, your numbers will continue to decrease and lead you to the inevitable reality of hard economic times for you and Parker. You came to me, knowing that something needs to change. Just because you have done something does not mean it is working; or if it has worked in the past, it doesn't mean it will continue to work. Look around; you're staying at one of the most expensive suites in Tahoe, and what type of pen is on that desk over there? That's right, it's a Cross. It should be a Parker. I cannot guarantee you that what I change will work, but I can guarantee you that if you continue along the current path, you will be forced to sell the company or it will be taken over, and my guess would be by Cross. Or we can re-think what you have done and go to the drawing board to bring Parker Pens back and relevant. Good luck to you and Parker Pens." Charlie got up from the table and proceeded to the door.

Robert stood up in bewilderment, eyes squinted and his mouth half open.

"One last parting thought Robert," Charlie added. "If your current campaign is doing fine and you're happy with your current numbers, then don't waste your time and mine. You didn't really think that I was going to just agree with your current strategy and tell you to hang in there, did you? These are different times my friend, and you can either change with them, or stay seated and use that Cross pen over there to sign your room service check." Charlie placed the documents on the table beside the door and walked out.

Wednesday. 1:15 p.m.

"Doris, what do I have at 1:30?" Charlie asked as he was in the car driving back to the office.

"I don't have anything for you until 3:00. That's the last scheduled appointment, because you need to get some rest before picking up Ray at the airport tonight. Is there something else you wanted done?" Doris responded.

"No, I just got done with Mr. Parker and wanted a real lunch. Place him as a potential, until he calls back. We'll revisit it in two months; please mark my calendar."

"I take it things didn't go so well? And what makes you so sure he will call you back?" Doris asked.

"He'll call back; it will just take a little thinking and evaluating on his part. He and the other board members will digest what I have said and call back. He may not have liked what I said, but give it a week and he'll call. I'll be at Rotchedo's for a while. Can you call ahead to make sure Frankie will be there? Do you want anything while I'm there?"

"No thank you. I just had leftovers, you're about 30 minutes too late!"

"Are there any messages that need my attention?" Charlie asked.

"I've taken care of your messages, except for one."

"One?" Charlie inquired.

"You had a strange call from someone named

Serina, she said she would call back later, and didn't

leave a call back number. She didn't say if it was

business or personal. She didn't say much, except to ask

for you."

"Serina called, and didn't say anything?" Charlie

asked, while trying to contain the little boy excitement in

his voice.

"I told you, she just asked if you were available,

and said she would call back; that was the extent of the

conversation. By the sound of your voice, you know

her? I've never heard that name before, nor have I

heard you that enthusiastic over someone I've never

heard of."

"I met her last month, but haven't heard from her

in a while. It's nothing. I'm just surprised she called. I'll

talk to you later." Charlie hung up the phone in a hurry,

feeling his heartbeat through his shirt.

Puzzled by the call, Charlie wondered how Serina found him. As he could recall, he had never given her his card or number. But this seemed to be par for the course with this woman. She seemed to show up out of the blue and leave the same way. She knew the cars he drove and private, unlisted phone numbers. This was deeply concerning to Charlie, but he was struggling with his emotions. Charlie was keenly aware of everything in his life. He controlled most everything he could, but with Serina, there were red flags at every corner. If it was anyone else, Charlie would call his security detail or the police, he was letting his guard down.

Thursday. 12:30 a.m.

After being awoken by the alarm, Charlie took a quick shower before heading off to the airport to pick up

Ray. Charlie had already arranged to have Frankie meet them at Rotchedo's for a drink, and to get caught up before heading back home. The flight was right on time and when it landed, five people got off. The last one to step off the plane was Ray. Landing at the Lake Tahoe airport was nothing glamorous. There were no terminals, no baggage claim, and no fancy security. The planes landed on a private airstrip, and stairs were rolled up to the door, if the plane did not have stairs themselves. When you exited the aircraft, you were out on the runway, and waited at the bottom of the stairs for your luggage to be unloaded from the belly of the plane. Primarily catering to private planes, the airport could not handle the landing of most commercial airliners. The largest planes to land here were commuter planes with around 35 seats.

Ray was a John Wayne, rugged type. He was 6'2,

with a muscular build and a shaved head that made him more intimidating. Sporting a grey beard and wearing his trademark dark Italian suit with his dress shirt unbuttoned at the top. Ray never went out in public without dress pants and a coat, but rarely wore a tie.

"Ray, you look good! Florida is taking good care of you. Welcome to Tahoe," Charlie greeted his old friend, with a big hug.

"Right back at you, my friend. It looks like Tahoe is treating you well. Sorry so late, but you can't beat the fare. I must watch my money now that I'm retired. Man, it is fucking cold here!" Ray said. Ray could afford to fly anywhere he wanted but was always careful where he spent his money.

Charlie had not seen Ray in ten years since the death of Charlie's parents. Charlie's parents died in a car accident on Christmas Eve. They were on their way to Charlie's house in Tahoe for a family getaway. After not showing up and no calls, Charlie called the police captain and they searched the roads around Tahoe. The weather that night had been bad. Tahoe had just gotten 48 inches of new snow, and that was only the first storm to hit. His parents wanted to beat the other storms, and since they did not like to fly, they drove everywhere. Unfortunately, the night they chose to drive was called "the storm of the century". Roads were closed, flights were canceled, and businesses were closed, including the many ski resorts.

After an all-night search with no luck, his parents were found on Christmas Day. They had lost control of their car and gone off the side of the road. The guardrail was broken in two. Both bodies had been ejected from the car and into the trees at the bottom of the cliff, where they had died on impact. The report stated that the car had spun out of control before hitting and breaking through the railing. The car fell about 50 feet to the bottom of the cliff. Both his parents had been wearing their seat belts, but the car had hit so hard and so fast, the belts were ripped from the bolts on the frame. They could not determine the exact speed they were traveling, but there were signs of skid marks before impact, meaning they were out of control when they hit the railing, or they tried to avoid hitting something. There was little chance of survival.

Charlie was very close to his parents, and held himself responsible for not sending his plane to get them. Although deep down he knew they would not have flown, Charlie still felt he could have prevented the accident. He was devastated. Soon after, he took a year off from Dean Witter to find some kind of peace. It was during this time that he developed and designed the concept for Rocklin and Roll Investments. During his leave, Charlie had to deal with his parents' estate in Las Vegas. He sold off the jewelry stores, house, and sold most of the furniture at auction, so there would be nothing left to remind him of his loss. The pictures and memories remained, but nothing else. Charlie would soon kick start his life into high gear on the heels of the death of his parents. Never looking back, he focused on his soon-to-be company. And that was the last time he had really seen Ray. They had since talked on the phone an average of once every couple of months, but never got around to spending some quality time. Charlie had seen Ray during a few business trips in Florida, but that was more of a meet and greet, rather than actually getting to sit down and talk about life. Until now.

Chapter Four

At Rotchedo's, Frankie was inside, lights on and food on the table when Charlie and Ray drove up in the Aston Martin. Just as Ray had requested, he was driving. Frankie greeted them at the door and gave Ray a hug.

Upon entering, Ray wasted no time sharing why he had flown up from Florida.

"This is a private affair, Charlie. I flew down here so I could talk to you in person, privately. This is a very sensitive issue, and one that should not be taken lightly. I prefer to talk to you alone. No disrespect to you Frankie; it's just a family thing." Ray briefed.

"No, I understand," Frankie said.

Looking at a puzzled Charlie, Frankie said in a

respectful yet unamused tone, "Charlie, it's alright, you know how to lock up when you leave. Just leave the dishes there and I'll have them cleaned up in the morning. I'll call you tomorrow, Charlie." Frankie walked out the door and locked it behind him.

"Ray, what are you doing? It is two in the morning. He came out to open this place up and feed us, and you treat him that way? I have known Frankie my whole life; he knows everything there is to know about me. Not a very good impression, having not seen you in a decade. Fuck, Ray, come on man," Charlie said, with annoyance.

"You're a man now, you can make your own decisions, and from what I have seen, you make pretty good decisions. If what I am about to tell you, you want to tell Frankie, then go ahead, but it will be your decision and it will not come back on me. Do you hear me? This is fucking serious. Nothing against Frankie, I love that man, but I love you more. I am not fucking around!"

Ray stood up and wiped his forehead that was moist. You could see the veins protruding through Ray's neck and the clinching of jaw muscles. In all the years Charlie had known Ray, serious was not something he had seen too often. Something was up. Ray was in trouble, and he could not hide it. Charlie awaited the bad news. Immediately, Charlie began to devise how he would help Ray. No matter what it was, he knew Ray would not take a handout, so Charlie had to come up with something creative.

"I came here to talk to you about your parents. Only you. Not Frankie, not over the phone, but to you, and in person."

Ray continued. "Last month, I got a visit from a detective by the name of Steve Tricks. He's a detective with the Las Vegas Police Department and came to visit me in Florida. He didn't call, he didn't send me an email; he got on a fucking plane and tracked me down in Florida. He asked me some questions about an incident that happened a long, long time ago. Which at that time I knew nothing about, and the same is true now, as far as anyone else is concerned. I am here to tell you, and only you. I want you to be aware, in case you are questioned, without you having to piece a puzzle together. This gets a little involved, so try and keep up."

Charlie got chills down the back of his neck. He felt his hair rise, as if someone was drawing a feather down his spine.

"Alright, you have my attention, Ray."

"OK, so Mr. Tricks wanted to know if I had heard anything from a Mary Rothwell within the past ten years. I had not. For the record, I do not know of any

Mary Rothwell, I told him. This Mrs. Rothwell had apparently died recently, and the detective was going through the formality of closing an old case, a case that has been lingering at the station for something like 40 years. I asked why the sudden interest in such an old case. I was informed that Mrs. Rothwell had insisted that the case be left open, in case there were any leads in solving the crime. He said it just like that: 'the crime'. As if I knew what the fuck he was talking about. When I asked what 'the crime' was, he said it was a murder; an unsolved, decades-old murder."

Ray took a drink of his whiskey while Charlie sat there with a bewildered look on his face, wondering where the hell this was leading. He listened intently to what Ray had to say, at times shaking his head as if he was listening to an open mic night of fiction from a favorite mystery writer.

"Mrs. Rothwell was in good with the Vegas Police ever since the death of her husband. She had been giving generously to the department, and in return they kept her file "open". Nothing has been done in this file for years, and now it was the duty of Tricks to close it out. It had been sitting on someone's desk, just waiting for this woman to die." Ray stopped.

"Do you follow me?"

"No, not really. I just don't understand what this has to do with me, my parents, or even you."

Charlie got up from the table and walked over to the door that led into the kitchen. Ray sat there in silence as he watched Charlie walk back over to the table. Raising a pint of Guinness to his lips, Charlie took in a huge gulp and sat back down, staring into Ray's eyes.

"Good, then you're listening. I take it that your

parents never mentioned the Rothwell's?"

"Rothwell? No, that name doesn't bring any memories. But I'm gathering that it should. I'm gathering that I'm not going to like what you are about to tell me." Charlie replied in a somber tone.

"By 1959, Sandy and Aaron had been in Vegas for three years and were doing very well. I was a rookie with the FBI, but I'll get to that later. Your parents met this couple and got to know them and would call them friends. They were good customers of the store, and had purchased a great deal of jewelry the year before. Something like $50,000 worth, and in 1959 that was a lot of fuckin' money. No one had that kind of money, not unless you were famous or connected in some way. Peter and Mary Rothwell were self-made millionaires, or so they said. It came out later that they had struck oil in Texas. They were living in this shit house and all of a sudden, this black stuff started coming up. Had to be

oil, in the middle of some small town in Texas."

"Sounds like something from the Beverly

Hillbillies!" Charlie commented.

"That is actually where the show comes from.

That show was made sometime in the early 60's, I think

around 62 if I am not mistaken, and was loosely of based

on Peter and Mary."

"You're kidding me."

"Listen, I'm not here to talk to you about the

fucking Beverly Hillbillies, fuck them. Forget about the

Hillbillies, that has nothing to do with what I am telling

you."

It was not often that Ray was all business. Once you got

to know him, he had quite the dry personality, but

today, he was not in the mood for any tomfoolery.

"Okay, sorry," Charlie said.

"You're starting to sound a little passionate about this story. I thought you had never heard of the Rothwells? I'm not sure I'm following you, Ray." Charlie added.

"If you remember, I said, as far as anyone else was concerned, I had never heard of these people. It is me and you here, no one else. Between me and you Charlie." Ray leaned in real close to Charlie and whispered, "Between me and you kid, I knew The Rothwells very well."
Charlie had no other option but to hear Ray out, no matter how much he wanted to leave and run.

"Where was I? Oh, in 59', I had known your parents for two years. I was a young kid, and had nowhere to go. It was your parents who helped me get into the academy. I owed them a great deal for that. They changed my life, and I've remained loyal ever since. It's not every day you meet people, who you can

trust with your life. People who are inherently good and

try and share that goodness, that was your parents.

From that point forward, I was indebted to them for life.

I was on a bad path, and they helped point me in the

right direction. I had no idea what I wanted or where I

wanted to go. I was in Vegas, hanging out with the

wrong kind of people, doing the wrong kind of things. I

was in one of their stores getting ready to rob them, and

that is when your father noticed something. He took me

aside and gave me some money. I ran away. Seriously, I

ran after he gave me $1000. The next day I returned.

Not to rob them or ask for more money, but to ask for a

job. I handed your father an envelope and returned the

money he had given me. I'm not sure what happened,

but I felt remorse. I knew I did not like where I was

headed." Ray paused to take a drink.

"That is when they introduced me to a gentleman who was an FBI agent. He recruited me into the FBI. After graduating from the academy, I stayed close with your parents, and this became a great friendship. They were like parents to me; I'm eternally grateful to them. I would lay down my life for them. I was there for whatever they wanted."

Charlie sat there in silence, eyes glued to Ray's mouth, waiting to hear more.

"Back to Peter and Mary. They came into the store one day, and took Sandy and Aaron out to lunch. When they returned, they all got into a car and drove to the bank. When I saw your parents the next day, they had told me that they had loaned the Rothwells $250,000. I was blown away. That is a lot of money today, not to mention 40 years ago. Can you imagine loaning someone $250k and they did not even know them for very long. What the fuck were they thinking?"

Ray stopped, took a drink of his whiskey and put his hands over his face, as if to rub off a spider web that had blown in from the outside.

Charlie was still entranced by the conversation and was sitting on the edge of his seat, wanting more. His Guinness was getting warm, and he hadn't moved.

"I asked them why they agreed to loan anyone that kind of money, but they seemed content with their decision. They said that the Rothwell's would pay it back within a year, with 50 percent interest. You and I both know that any deal that is too sweet, is not a good deal, but money is enticing. Your parents were not the gullible kind, so I was still trying to understand why they would loan that kind of money to people they had only known for a couple of years. But I figured they did not get where they were at, by making bad financial decisions.

As the year went by, we saw less and less of Peter and Mary. They had stopped coming into the store, and stopped spending money to pay off their accounts, like they used to. Your father tried on several occasions, with and without me, to call and stop by their place, but could never get a hold of anyone. Then after two years, in 1961, they came into the store. Peter and Mary walked into the store and handed your parents a check in the amount of $25,000. When your father asked where the rest was, they said there would be no more. That was all that was loaned to them, and they are returning the full amount. They wanted nothing more to do with them." Charlie interrupted.

"Wait a minute. I thought the amount was $250,000, not $25,000."

"It was $250,000." Ray answered.

"Then I'm confused. Why did Peter and Mary only repay $25,000?"

"Because my friend, they did not have the money, or they did not want to give it back. Who really knows? Maybe they lost the initial 250 thousand, and did not want to admit their loss. I know they had money, they struck fucking oil! In any event, the check they gave your parents was in the amount of 25,000, I saw it."

"Who's to say that my parents did not only give them $25,000? How can you be certain that they gave the Rothwell's $250,000?" Charlie asked.

"I have known your parents long enough, and that isn't the type of people they were. They had no reason to lie, not to me. I knew everything about them and what they did. If they said it was $250,000, then it was. Plus, I'd seen what they had laying around and if it really was 25k, they could have just gotten it out of the safe, that was petty cash to them Charlie. The only reason they ever went to the bank was for large amounts of cash," Ray responded.

"So, Rothwell gave my parents $25,000 and called it even."

"That's right. Your father asked where the rest was, and again Peter denied that the original amount was $250,000. That was when your father took me aside and brought me the bank receipt for a cash withdrawal for $250,000 on August 5, 1959. I was satisfied. Your father went back out to talk to Peter, but they just turned around and walked out, with nothing more to say."

"I still don't understand where the detective and police come in. Did I miss something?" Charlie asked.

"No, you haven't missed anything, kid." Ray said with the glass of whiskey in his hand. He took a drink, his upper lip was shining in the light, glistening with a light coat of Blanton's that remained. Ray wiped his mouth with the back of his hand and put down the glass. He took a deep breath.

"After they had walked out, I noticed your parents and the look of betrayal and disappointment in their eyes. I could not stand by and let them feel this way; not after what they did for me. I told you they saved me. Before I ever met your parents, I was a bad kid, I was underground. I did underground crimes for money. I was making some pretty good money for some big hitters. I was connected, in a way. But with that connection, came a very big price, and I was ready to get out, I just needed a reason. Your parents gave me that reason. They took me in and gave me a vision to change my ways. When they came to Vegas, they were introduced to some pretty influential people. People you just don't meet on the corner of the Las Vegas Boulevard.

These were people who were responsible for the Vegas

you know today. They made some calls, for me. And

then next thing I knew, I was in the academy. I was out,

just like I wanted to be. As I said, they did for me what

any parent would do for their own child."

"The one thing I did not lose was my

connections. I may have been a federal agent, but I

remained loyal to those I had worked for. I went to your

father and talked about some possible solutions. One of

those solutions was, to make Peter Rothwell disappear.

At the time, I was not worried about the consequences;

all I wanted was revenge, and it was something that I

was familiar with. I wanted to do something for your

dad, just as he had done for me. Call it payback. Call it

getting even. Call it a favor. After a lengthy discussion

and a lot of convincing, he told me to do what I needed

to do. He would put it in my hands to deal with Peter Rothwell, in any way that I saw fit."

"Are you saying what I think you are saying?" Charlie asked.

"Charlie, the time was right. I owed this to your father. Times now are not at all what they were. You couldn't get away with that today. Shit, you can't even walk across the street today without someone watching you or recording it. I decided to call an old friend of mine, his name was 'Ice'. I met with Ice on a Friday and by Monday, everything had been taken care of. Peter was never going to repay another cent of money, so he just disappeared. And that is the way we left it. We never thought about it again, and we never discussed it, ever!"

"What do you mean? What did you do, Ray? I cannot possibly be hearing you correctly. You did not just tell me that you, that my parents, eliminated someone. They called a hit on someone. Rothwell?" Charlie said with a shaken voice.

It was 3:30 a.m., and there came a knock on the front door. Charlie and Ray could not see the door from where they were sitting, so they just let it go and continued to talk. But the knocking didn't go away. For the next five minutes, it continued. First it was a single knock. Then a pause, followed by another knock. Charlie ran his hands through his hair and glared at Ray. This person whom he had known his whole life, and his parents, Charlie did not really know any of them. Charlie did not want to understand. As the knock got louder, Charlie got up from the table to look around the corner towards the door. And there she was. Serina was standing there in a white tank top with a blue skirt, waiting to be let in.

"I don't believe it; I haven't seen this girl in weeks, and she just shows up here, now? Out of nowhere, she always knows when to just show up." Charlie said.

He walked toward the door to let Serina in.

"Charlie don't do that; you need to hear this. This is a matter of life and death. Charlie, don't open that door," Ray pleaded, but to no avail.

Charlie opened the door and Serina walked in, watching Charlie with every step. Charlie introduced Serina to Ray, and laid the keys to the Aston Martin on the table.

"Ray, take the car to the house, the address is in the nav, in case you need it. I will see you later, and we can finish catching up." Charlie was done listening to Ray. No matter what Ray had said or what he was going to say, Charlie was done. He was not going to let Serina leave again. Charlie walked Ray to the front door, gave

him a quick hug and turned to Serina. Ray did not say a

word, he did not even say goodbye. He looked at the

keys in his hand, got into the car and drove off, leaving a

cloud of dust.

Walking back into the restaurant, Charlie looked

into Serina's eyes. She was the most beautiful thing he

had ever laid his eyes on. Charlie had fallen, and hard.

There was no one he wanted more right now, and there

she was. And he did not even know her last name.

"How did you find me here?" Charlie asked.

"I was just driving by, and saw your car. I

figured I should stop in to say 'Hi'. Was that alright, or

would you like me to go?" Serina asked in a low but

sensual voice.

"You mean leave, again? No, of course not. But

how did you know what kind of car I drive?"

"Remember, I saw you drive up at Windsor Steak House months ago. You couldn't keep your eyes off of me. Are you telling me that you don't remember that day?"

Charlie did remember Windsor Steak House and remembered it well. That was the second time he had seen Serina after meeting her at the Club. He was outside on the phone waiting for his lunch appointment to arrive, when Serina walked by. Charlie arrived first, he remembered that. In the back of his mind, he knew he was not driving his Aston Martin and he knew something was a little off about Serina and what she knew about him, but that didn't matter. In business, Charlie will call your bullshit immediately, but with Serina, he is not so harsh. He did not want to lose this chance of getting to know her, so he is taking every interaction in stride.

Serina and Charlie got into her car and drove off.

With no particular place to go, they just talked and drove

for most of the night, or at least what was left of it. At

about 6:30, they decided to go back to Charlie's place.

Without even telling Serina which direction to go, she

knew exactly where he lived. They were going to end up

there, no matter what happened that evening. Upon

their arrival, the Aston Martin was in the garage and

there was a note on the boot of the car.

"C- You need to call me! Don't trust her, trust

me! Call me soon." It was signed "R".

Charlie took the note, folded it and put it in his

back pocket. With a smile, he showed Serina inside.

They made their way to the main entrance to the house.

Impressed with the double staircase leading up to the

second level, Serina took one side and Charlie the other.

With each step, their passion was building. At the top of

the staircase, Charlie picked her up and led her to the

master bedroom where the French Doors were open to

the outside. On the patio overlooking the lake, water

was running from the fountain into the hot tub. They

both started to undress, and Charlie led the way onto the

patio. The jets were on, and the foam was rich. Bodies

in motion, water was splashing over the sides, just as

Charlie had been dreaming about. Serina's eyes were

closed, as if telling herself to enjoy the moment.

Morning came with a ring of the phone, and

Doris was on the other end.

"Charlie, do you realize what time it is? 9:00 a.m.

Are you alright?" Doris asked in a concerned voice.

"No, I'm just fine. It was a late night, and Ray

had to go back to Florida. I lost track of time. I'll be in

within the hour."

Doris had already received a message from Ray.

She knew Ray had left earlier that morning.

Charlie turned to Serina and kissed her forehead before getting up to shower.

"I have to go to the office now. Will you be here when I get home?" Charlie asked as he was standing naked in front of the bathroom entrance.

"Do you want me here when you get home?"

"I want you to meet me for dinner, and then I'll bring you back home. I'll have a car waiting for you this afternoon to take you. And you won't be alone in the house, there will be people around to help you if you need it." Out of character for someone like Charlie to leave a total stranger in his house. He knew that, and his brain was yelling at him, but he wouldn't listen. He didn't want to chance Serina leaving again.

Charlie went off to work and got a late start to another busy Friday.

"Charlie, welcome." Doris said with a smile. It took everything she had not to ask or say anything to Charlie. She had to respect his decisions. Doris did not know the details of Serina; only that Ray warned her to look out for Charlie. This was not the Charlie she had known for the past five years; something about him was different. Doris knew that look on his face; a look that only a woman would know.

"Charlie, Richard Keller will be in at 10:00 a.m. to go over the six-month report on his company, and you have an early lunch scheduled today to meet with Bill Gates. He's in town for a chess tournament, and wanted to see you. After that you'll need to catch the plane to Butte, to meet with Ted Turner about selling some of his assets and creating a new non-profit. He would also like to run a few things by you about your partnership. He has invited you to stay the night, so I moved all your other appointments to Monday and Tuesday of next week. You can be back here by Saturday afternoon." Doris rested.

Charlie sat in the chair behind his desk, staring off, looking at nothing in particular. Doris continued, "You need to call back James on the cover for the book. He has sent over some profile pictures that he wants to use; this needs to be finalized to go to print. He also sent over two distribution contracts that he needs you to sign. Also, before you meet with Keller, call Ray; he has called twice. He didn't call you at home because he wanted to talk to you in private."

"That all sounds fine. Can you please send five dozen roses to my house to the attention of 'Ms. Serina.' Also, have Serina go to see Paul, and have him set her up with something nice to wear for Saturday morning. I would like to send the jet to pick her up and fly her out to the Turners' late tonight. Call Ted to see if that will be alright. Please make arrangements for Saturday morning; I would like to take Serina out, just the two of us. Ask Ted where he would recommend for a romantic evening. We can then return late Saturday night. Thanks Doris."

Charlie got up and walked toward the window with a huge smile on his face, thinking about the upcoming weekend.

This was the first time Doris had heard Charlie mention a woman's name, and three times in a row. Doris had been around long enough to know when she should ask questions, and when she should stay quiet. This was a time when she would stay quiet, waiting for Charlie to give more information.

Chapter Five

The Desert Inn Hotel and Casino, a paradise mecca in the middle of the desert, was the main reason high-profile clientele went to Vegas. When Frank Sinatra decided to perform in Las Vegas, it was not at the Sahara, the Sands or the Horseshoe Club, it was at the Desert Inn. The hotel opened in 1950 and has almost tripled its earnings year after year. The Rocklin's were fortunate to have an opportunity to own a store inside the DI. In 1957, the first Tiffin's Jewelers, which was what the Rocklin's named their store, opened in the Desert Inn, and it was a good year. After only a year, 1958 saw the opening of the second store. Beating their initial projections, the DI store made over 15 million dollars. Money went a long way in 58', and the

Rocklins were pulling in five hundred thousand a month, after expenses and paying their share to the casino. The high-priced items did not stay in the windows long enough to collect dust, and the inventory was being turned over every two weeks. That was a problem, but a good problem to have.

People were no longer going to Vegas just to gamble; they were going to see entertainment and shopping. With entertainers, you find money, and with the money, you find expensive items. Special orders did not seem so special when you are ordering them five and ten at a time. Pieces that would usually go on consignment, would be put in the window on Monday, and be sold by Tuesday. If you needed a piece of jewelry or to design something unique, everyone knew where to go. The word around town about the Rocklin's store was spreading so quickly, that people were coming to the Desert Inn just to shop in their store. It was not just

the quality of the jewelry; it was their clientele.

Not only did Tiffin's carry top of the line in

watches and diamonds, they had one of the most

decorated and talented jewelers in the business. Gary

was fresh out of college with a degree in architecture

design and wanted to pursue hotel and casino design.

When the Desert Inn could not hire him, they referred

him to the Rocklins. Not yet knowing his true calling,

Gary learned by watching Aaron. Fascinated with

jewelry design, he was hooked. After only a year, all

you had to do was give him an idea of what you wanted,

and he created it. He would put it on paper, then make a

mold of the design and brought it to life with gold and

platinum. This guy was so good that other jewelry

stores as far as New York were calling for custom-made

pieces. He made rings, necklaces and designed pendants

for the rich and famous all over the world. The phone was constantly ringing for repairs and custom pieces to go with the lights and glam of Las Vegas.

Tiffin's was now a household name in Vegas, and owners of the other major casinos wanted a piece of the action. Moe Dalitz, owner of the DI, became aware of these interests and thus began protection of the Rocklins. Being approached by other casinos was a great position to be in, but there was a price. In Vegas, you had to be very careful who you talked with and who you dealt with. Vegas was a place ruled by an elite few, and those few were very powerful men. Only with permission directly from Moe and the other owners, could the Rocklins talk to the other casinos. Under an exclusive re-negotiated agreement, the Rocklins and Dalitz began to charge a fee to use the name of the store, in addition to being a part owner of the stores that went into other casinos.

Franchising was nothing new; fast food

restaurants had been doing this for years. Tiffin's was

the first so-called franchise that branched out outside of

the McDonald's and Wendy's. Mr. Dalitz had so much

influence and power over the other owners, that the

original agreement in 56' was declared invalid. Moe took

care of those who took care of him. You could not look

at the Rocklins without having to ask Moe first. Tiffin's

Jeweler's was now the 'franchise' store and others were

free to use it, with conditions of course. As long as the

DI, Moe and the Rocklins got a piece of the action, it was

all yours. That franchise fee was somewhere in the range

of $500,000 to one million, just to secure the name,

which did not include stock or percentages of ownership,

and profits from the store. The mastermind behind the

exclusive agreements was Moe and his attorneys. No

matter how many other Tiffin's stores were out there, the

DI remained the premier store.

Over the next few years, the Rocklins opened up

five other stores in the neighboring casinos, with them

and Dalitz owning 51%. By the end of 1962, Tiffin's

collectively, was bringing in roughly ten million a month,

but not all of that went to the Rocklins. There were many

hands in the pot that needed to get paid.

Aaron believed that first impressions were

everything, and that is what people kept coming back

for. With every store you walked into, you could see

some of the custom pieces that were made for some of

the biggest names in the entertainment industry. At the

Sahara location, you could find the solid gold and

diamond glasses made for Elton John and Elvis Presley.

At the Dunes location, were the six carat matching rings

that were made for Sinatra and Sammy Davis, Jr. And at

the DI location, were the necklace and bracelet made for

Marilyn Monroe, as requested by President, John F.

Kennedy. Although most of the income came from

custom pieces, the Rocklins wanted Tiffin's to remain a "family" business to the locals. In 1959, Sandra and Aaron took stock in two of their clients, the Rothwells. Mary and Peter Rothwell had come into the store a few times, and purchased some high-priced watches and necklaces: an 18k solid gold Vacheron Constantin limited edition watch, his and hers, along with two Herringbone 14k gold chains. After they spent over $75,000 in the store, the Rocklins decided to dedicate more time to the relationship. This was in part a business decision as well as personal.

Mary and Peter Rothwell were great customers. They did not rank in the same level as Presley or Sinatra, but they were real, salt of the earth people. The Rocklins were always friendly to their customers, but the rule was never mix business with personal. Sandra and Aaron knew the rules, no matter how much they seemed to connect with a customer, but the Rothwells were different, or so they thought. You would never tell a friend who was behind on their payments, "no", or at least it would not be easy. But a non-paying customer, you could say "no," without a second thought. There was nothing to lose in that relationship. The Rocklins knew the line but crossed over anyway.

The Rothwell's did not live in Vegas, so they only saw them on occasion. But something was different with this couple; it was as if they had known each other for years, something just clicked. Over the next ten months, the Rocklins and Rothwells took many trips together. They had gone on cruises, safaris and train trips all over the world. They had a lot in common: both liked fine dining, purchasing expensive gifts, taking lavish vacations, and both had plenty of money. When you meet someone and can talk for hours on end about nothing in particular. When you can sit with someone

else on a long car ride, and there is not an awkward

moment of silence. When you can talk to someone about

anything and everything, without having to worry about

what they might say in return or place judgment. This

was that kind of relationship.

Aaron and Sandy have worked hard to get to

where they are at, but the Rothwells discovered them,

literally overnight. They had been living in Texas, both

working for the US Postal Service. Peter and Mary had

two children, and were set to retire in twenty years, if

they stayed with the government. Then in 1955,

something happened that changed the way they looked

at life. They purchased their house in 1945 and planned

to die in that house. In 1955, their family was growing

and needed more space, so Peter decided to add on to

the house, instead of spending the money on another

house. Rather than hire a contractor to do the addition to the house, Peter did it himself. It might take a little longer, but the savings would be worth it.

Just as he began to dig, the tractor hit something beneath the surface. It was only about twenty feet below the ground, but a small amount of black liquid started emerging from the ground. Thinking it was oil from the tractor, Peter continued to dig. Then suddenly from under the tractor came a fountain of black liquid. Peter knew it was not coming from the tractor any longer, and realized he had struck oil. The Rothwell's instantly became millionaires.

Once you discover newfound wealth, others seem to discover you as well. Friends began to come out of the woodwork, and suddenly, everyone knew them or wanted to get to know them. The Rothwells became a household name in Texas. When you acquire that kind of money, your life changes. The way you think

changes. The way you treat other people, changes.

There are those out there who can handle this kind of

fame, but for the Rothwells, arrogance would not even

begin to describe them. They turned into arrogant

assholes.

Peter, Mary and their two children moved to the

elite suburb of Terrace West; an exclusive and reclusive

area that contained 50 homes and a private lake. They

purchased a 10,000-square-foot house on a lake and got

two new cars. Their children no longer went to public

schools. They enrolled them in the best-rated private

school and so what if it was two hundred miles away,

round-trip. They both retired early to spend more time

with their kids. Trips to exotic places became more

accessible and vacations were never a matter of not

having enough money. The Rothwells looked at

discovering oil like they deserved it or were entitled to it. Peter and Mary were now too good for some of their old friends and they let everyone know it.

Peter and Mary took many mini-vacations; a weekend getaway to Scottsdale, one to Palm Springs and some to Santa Barbara. Las Vegas was a great place to visit, but never to live. Every time the Rothwells went to Vegas, they stayed at the Desert Inn. They would get their rooms complementary because of the amount of money they played in the casino. They would usually travel on a Friday, stay for two nights, and come home Sunday. They did this twice a month. On an average, gaming for them was good. Playing was a matter of how much you wanted to invest. If your investment was high, the probability of winning increased. And when you play as much as they did, you won a lot. And when you win a lot, you learn to report what you want to report. Once you win a certain amount in gambling, you are required to report it to the IRS as income. If you know the system well enough, you can report loses as well as winnings and make them cancel each other out, that way, your taxable amount of winnings would be limited to a small amount, if any. They became very good at taking advantage of the system.

Peter loved craps; that was his game. He did not mess around with any of the slots or video poker, those were not fast enough for him or the stakes weren't high enough. He liked the dice action and the ability to control your own bet. With craps, there is some skill involved, unlike the slots. He mostly stuck to the Don't Pass/Don't Come and the Horn Bet, and dabbled in the field, but knew when to walk away. Statistically, your best odds are at the craps table, just so as long as you don't start playing the field. Peter, for the most part, stuck to the odds. As for Mary, she stuck with the slots and video poker tournaments. Every week the Desert Inn would hold an invitation only slot tournament to its high rollers, and Mary was one of them. You pay an entry fee and play several rounds, usually consisting of twenty minutes each. At the end of the round, your total monies are added up and then you are ranked with the other participants. That was it. No skill, just luck. Not much thought process goes into a slot tournament, and Mary was not one to think much anyway.

Chapter Six

For two months, Charlie and Serina had been virtually inseparable. Every night when Charlie comes home, Serina is there to greet him, and every morning before Charlie goes to work, Serina is there by the front door with a kiss. Not only was Charlie smiling when he went to work, but also when he came home, and that was foreign for him. He was a relatively happy person, but now he actually comes home when it is still light outside. Saturdays were no longer spent in the office, but at home or on a plane taking Serina on a surprise trip. Charlie did not believe in love, it was a weakness, a distraction. Love was that fantasy that everyone wanted, but it was just far enough out of reach that you could never quite get your hands around it. Love was a killer.

Love clouded the mind, skewed the decision-making process, and introduces emotions into places it did not belong. At least that was the way Charlie use to feel. Love seemed to change the priorities of business, but now he was starting to become a believer in this thing called "love".

During the week, Serina would go home after seeing Charlie off to work, to get a new change of clothes for the next day.

"This is silly; you go home every day, when you're here every day. Instead of just having a dresser, why don't you move in?" Charlie asked.

"Move in, here? Do we really know each other that well? I love you, I really do, and you make every dream come true, but I'm not ready for that, not just yet." This was her reply every time Charlie would bring up the subject. Charlie was ready though. She was everything he was looking for in a woman. Serina was beautiful, she was witty, she made him smile, and she was smart. She was even able to talk business strategies, diversity and inclusion and culture. He wasn't sure how she knew this, but she did. Serina on the other hand, was not thinking about moving in.

Business remained priority number one, but Serina was a close second and closing in fast to the top spot. Charlie still met with clients and spoke at different engagements, but the extended lengthy trips were no longer, and speaking events were determined by the location and Serina's availability. The 200 return calls a day that Charlie had built his business on, soon became 50 calls a day or he delegated to someone in his office. And his hours were beginning to look like bankers' hours. Charlie was beginning to turn down referrals from other clients, because there wasn't enough time to spend with Serina. Serina never asked him to not go on

a trip, or to come home early; she didn't have to. She

knew the power she had over Charlie and without

speaking a word. At this point in their relationship, she

didn't ask for much, and never put demands on Charlie.

She appeared to be the perfect companion. If Charlie

wanted to meet for lunch on short notice, she was

available. If they wanted to go out of town for the

weekend, she packed their bags. If Charlie wanted sex,

she was available for whatever he had in mind.

No one could remember the last time Charlie

took a day off of work, let alone two days off. Doris

could not even think of one time this had happened since

she has been working for him. Now that Serina was in

the picture, he has amended his schedule to a four-day

work week. He was either gone every Friday or called in

on Mondays. Last month they went to the wine county

in Napa California, spent a weekend off the coast of
Oregon, and attended the Shakespeare festival in
Ashland. This month they have already traveled to San
Francisco and stayed at the Ritz and Half Moon Bay, also
at the Ritz. Never before had Charlie enjoyed his life this
much. He was able to travel to places and relax, without
the rushing to meetings or lectures or phone calls. He
was actually taking a vacation; a new word in his
vocabulary, and he was beginning to fall deeply in love
with Serina.

Serina knew everything there was to know about
Charlie, because he told her. She heard about his
parents, their accident, his first job out of college, his lack
of relationships, when he made his first hundred million.
Serina kept asking, and he kept talking. Even when she
didn't ask, he just talked. There was always something
to talk about. It could be as unpretentious as a movie, or

as occupying as the death penalty or abortion. Their

relationship came easy for Charlie, and he felt as if he

had met his soulmate. On the other side of the table

Serina, never talked about herself. Charlie didn't even

know the names of her parents, where she grew up, or if

she had any siblings. But he didn't care. Serina was

there with him now, and that was all that mattered. He

was so busy talking about himself or engaging in

meaningless conversation that he never really thought

about asking Serina questions about her past. Then

again, she never offered to talk about herself. When

Charlie did ask a personal question about her past, she

quickly diverted the conversation to something about

him, and he went along with it. Call it selfish or

egotistical, he didn't care. Time seemed to stand still

when he was with Serina. Charlie wanted every

moment, to last forever.

"Cancel my 9:00, and call the airport to make arrangements for Serina and I to leave at 10:00 to go to Seattle." Charlie told Doris on Monday morning.

"An extra-long weekend? I'll have the plane waiting for you. And when will you be returning? Should I cancel tomorrow's meeting with the board?"

"No. We'll be back this evening; we're just going up for the day. Going to have lunch and do some shopping in Bellevue. I will be at the 7:30 meeting in the morning. Thanks."

So, they were off, yet again on another little excursion. This was becoming the norm for Charlie. There was no doubt that this thing called "love" was definitely clouding his mind. For someone who was so against love and adamant that is was the root of all evil, he was becoming the world's largest hypocrite. And that was starting to concern Doris.

The last time Doris had to cancel or reschedule a meeting for Charlie was when his plane couldn't take off out of the Chicago airport due to snow and heavy winds, and that was four years ago. Since Serina entered the picture, Doris has been canceling meetings at least once a week. Although she didn't mention it to Charlie, she felt that something was not right. No one, could have this much of an effect on a man, especially if that man was Charlie Rocklin. As long as Charlie was happy and the business wasn't suffering due to his absence, Doris kept it to herself and let fate take care of the rest. But a problem was starting to appear. Referrals were coming in at an alarming rate and now, Charlie got roughly one per week. The average monthly revenue that was being deposited had dropped over 50% in the past three months. Doris was not the only one concerned with Charlie's actions and new way of life.

Not that it ever crossed Charlie's mind, but Serina never worked. She never had to "go home" anymore, and never called anyone, like a parent or a best friend. Serina was always available for Charlie. She answered her phone on the first ring, as if she was always expecting a call. She never seemed to have any problems with the plans, or voice too much of an opinion, but Charlie was too caught up in his infatuation.

Chapter Seven

Tuesday

"Ray, how the hell are you? Long time no hear." Charlie said in a cheery voice.

"So, there you are. I have been calling you for the past two fucking months and have not heard from you. Do you know how many times I drove to the fucking airport to get on a plane to see if you were alright? We need to talk. I'm not sure how long you're going to avoid talking about this. This is not for me my brother, trust me! And it isn't like you to not return my calls. Is everything alright? Are you in trouble?" he asked.

"No, everything could not be better. Business is great, and I'm really enjoying life right now. I think I have found a good balance Ray." Charlie bragged.

"You are starting to 'enjoy life', what the fuck

does that mean? Who is this? You know, I almost hate to say this, but it sounds like that girl is taking you for a ride and one you better get off real soon." Ray said in a somewhat angry yet concerned voice.

"Yes, I met a girl. She's the one who came to the restaurant that night we were talking, remember? Her name is Serina. I really like this girl, Ray. When I'm at work, I cannot stop thinking about her. When I'm at home looking in her eyes, I cannot stop thinking about her. Yeah, I haven't called you back because I've been with Serina. Sorry man, I really am, but I just don't want to lose her. She is truly amazing. There are no complaints from me, not a single one!"

"Well, I have a single fucking complaint Charlie. You get a little piece of ass, and you let it run your life. I have never seen you act this way, not even when you made ten million dollars in one day. You have known her for what, two fucking months, maybe three? Are

you kidding me? You don't really think you know this

girl, do you? Where did she come from? How did you

meet? Does she have a big family? Did a friend

introduce you, or did she just appear out of the fucking

sky on your doorstep? I bet you don't even know her

last name. What's her last name, Charlie? You are a

very wealthy man and I could name a dozen women

who would do exactly what this woman is doing. She is

taking you down man. This is NOT the Charlie I know,

or maybe the Charlie I really don't want to know." Ray

cautioned.

"Where is this coming from? And who are you to

tell me how to run my life? What are you trying to say?

Because for once in my life, I can see a future with a

woman, and someone other than just myself. I can see

her as the mother of my children, and you are criticizing

my judgment. Sure, I have always been focused on the company and have given it all I have, but now I need to look at the bigger picture, I need to enjoy what I have worked so hard for. I love Serina. I really do. She's the first woman who does not look at me for my money and treats me like no other woman has before. We can talk for hours, and still have something to say to one another. We have so much in common, at least I think we do Ray. God damnit man, what gives you the right to tell me who or what I should see and when? You don't even know her!"

"Neither do you Charlie. Listen, I'm just telling you to slow down and take a look at the situation. Find a little out about your Serina. Just because she's sleeping with you, does not mean that she is your soul mate. She may be the one, but keep focus on what is important to you and don't lose sight of that. That is what makes you who you are. Your ability to keep track of everything in your life with so much going on. Just be careful, that's all, just be careful." said Ray.

"I can take care of myself, but I appreciate your thoughts."

"Charlie, I still need to talk to you. Come down to Florida, tomorrow. Alone." Ray pleaded.

"You will not let that go? What's the urgency in all this? What is so damn important that you can't tell me over the phone?"

"Charlie, do you remember any of our last conversation? This is serious shit, brother. You need to talk to me, no bullshit. This shit is real. What I told you was only the beginning and I do fear that there is more to come. Something or someone is out there, you need to be a little extra cautious right now."

"You want me alone? Okay my man. I hear you,

and if you say it is important, then it is important. I can

make arrangements for some meetings in Florida with

clients and can come talk to you. How does tomorrow

or the day after sound? I haven't been down there in a

little while; I am sure I can make that happen."

"Let's make it the day after tomorrow, Thursday.

I'll meet you at the private hangers for people like you

who don't fly commercial. See you in a few days, and

please just watch yourself, and for God sake, please

come alone. That means, you and only you, brother."

Wednesday

Wednesday was looking to be a very busy day

for Charlie. If he was going to go down to Florida on

Thursday, then Wednesday needed to encompass two

days of work. Charlie arrived at the office at 4:30 in the

morning, and found his calendar on his desk opened to

the day with everything that was scheduled, including a

working lunch. Just as she does every night before she leaves, Doris prepares the following day for Charlie. Charlie has his schedule in Outlook and in a daily planner as a backup. When Doris arrived at 8:00, Charlie had already returned the 50 phone calls that were listed in his OneNote. He had just finished up a video conference meeting with a potential client in Japan, a start-up with five hundred million in cash reserves that had not turned out one tangible product. Had a board meeting for his non-profit, providing under-privileged graduating seniors with college tuition and computers if they attended one of the two local Nevada state universities. A mentoring session with his mentor, Warren Buffet; and a brief call with Arrow Rowland. Charlie had met Arrow years ago when he first met Victor Shallows and since Victor's death, Charlie and Arrow have remained close.

Doris makes her way into see Charlie, as she does every morning for the daily "sit-down." The agenda is always the same, to review the current day for any changes and review the next day for planning. If there are any business-critical decisions that need to be made for the day, they are discussed here.

"We got the retainers and fees for last month; they are down from the previous month. We collected just over two hundred thousand in two weeks, down from the previous two weeks. It was in line what we collected last period." Doris wanted to say so much, but she has learned to keep her comments to herself until asked.

Just as Doris went into another statement, Charlie interrupted her.

"I need to get these numbers to where they need to be, I know that."

Without missing a beat, Doris continued, as if Charlie had not spoken a single word.

"On your OneNote, I have provided the breakdown of the retainers. There is a story being done about you for *Time* magazine and they would like to interview you later this afternoon. You are open at 2:30 for 15 minutes, I have added this to the calendar. *Forbes* also called and would like to write a follow up piece from last year. They are sending me the details and we will discuss once I get them. They would like to propose a yearly follow-up, a new concept of following a company and its success, again, details and we will discuss. Meg from HP called and left her number but nothing else, said you would know. At 9:00 you need to go to Harrah's to meet with Bennett about their expansion, reserves, allocation and 180 day plan, that will take up to 11:30. From there you should get some lunch or I can order in for you. Starting at 12:30, you will be in back-to-back meetings here until 8:00 tonight. I have left a half hour in between your 3:00, 4:30 and 5:30 for phone calls." Doris took a deep breath.

"Sounds fine. And thank you for keeping everything in order here the last few months. Did I mention that I'll be going to Florida tomorrow? If you can, please set up some meetings with clients down there."

"You said something about it yesterday, and I called Ray to get the details. And I already took the liberty in setting up appointments with some of your clients down there. I will let you know if they are available and put them in Outlook. Tentatively, I have blocked out 1:00 to 4:00. I'll get you the details later this afternoon."

"Doris, you are awesome. I really don't know

what I would do without you. Let me ask you something. Have you noticed a difference in me the past few months?" Charlie said as he looked out the window, obviously preoccupied.

This is when Doris could provide her true feelings and observations, but she kept it clean. Bills were still getting paid, payroll was still being made, and money was still coming in, although not as much as in the previous years. Doris was respectful in her response.

"The only difference I have seen is that smile on your face that never goes away. And really, you are always very appreciative of my work, but these past two months, you have been exceptionally complimentary!"

Doris always knew the right thing to say and when to say it.

Thursday

Charlie's plane took off from The Lake Tahoe

airport at 4:00 a.m., and got him into Miami, Florida at around 11:30 a.m., Florida time. Just as Ray had promised, he was there on the private tarmac standing against his car, waiting as Charlie's jet landed. The sky was deep blue, and the sun was glowing bright with the humidity at 90%. Perfect for a light pair of slacks and a short sleeve shirt, but Charlie walked down the stairs of the plane dressed in a custom Brioni three-piece suit, ready for business. Ray, on the other hand, was there in a pair of board shorts, a half buttoned up Hawaiian short sleeve shirt, a flat hat, and flip-flops.

"Good morning," he said to Ray.

"Listen, just so you know, I have a 1:00 and a 3:00 today. You can have me before and after, but I need to make it to these meetings. Can we work around that?"

"Not a problem, I'm just happy you could make the time to see me," Ray said as he gave Charlie a big bear hug.

Charlie walked past Ray. Ray stood there for a moment as if someone else was going to exit the plane. No one followed and Ray was pleased.

The men got into Ray's 2015 convertible Miata and headed for Mt. Morris. The bar was a hangout for the young kids on Friday and Saturday nights, but on a Thursday mid-morning, there will be no one around. Ray wanted total privacy. As they drove to Morris, about twenty minutes from the airport, Ray went over what they had discussed a few months earlier at Rotchedo's. Going over it for a second time, Charlie was still unable to make the connection and urgency of the conversation. What did any of this have to do with him, and why has it taken so long for Ray to bring it up, and why is it so private?

After Ray parked the car and shut off the engine,

he turned to Charlie.

"Now, where were we? Tricks, the Vegas detective, came to see me over the Rothwell thing. Rothwell had disappeared some time ago, and this was just a formality when a case is closed. The amount in question was $250,000, and not $25,000. Peter did not want to return the whole amount; shit, for that matter, he completely denied the full amount. That really pissed me off. Did I touch on Jansen yet?" Ray asked Charlie.

"Yeah, a little, maybe. You had mentioned that you called an old friend, who I am thinking is Jansen and he took care of something. That is what I don't quite follow. What was taken care of?"

"Jansen, my old buddy, murdered Peter Rothwell for your father."

Silence filled the air as Charlie sat in the passenger seat, his door open, staring at Ray. After what appeared to be several minutes, but really the longest 10 seconds of his life, Charlie finally took a big gasp of the Floridian air. It was as if he was sucker-punched in the kidneys and had the wind knocked out of him. He could feel his heart skip a beat, again, and again, and again. Charlie ran his hands through his hair and could feel himself tremble. He could barely muster a word. He began to open and close his right hand; a numbness had fallen over his extremities. Open and close, open and close.

"Are you…" with a slight pause. "Are you telling me that my father is a murderer? My father killed someone. Is that what you just told me? He had someone killed. This is insane. Fucking insane." Charlie said in a stern tone, as he stood up out of the car. Ray, who was still calmly sitting in the driver's seat with his door closed. He exited the car, and walked toward

Charlie, who had not moved. Raising his right hand and placing it on Charlies shoulder, Ray tried to explain his last bombshell of a sentence.

"Your father did not kill anyone; Jansen did it. Jansen did me and your father a big favor. Peter was a problem, and it was not right what he had done. I knew that, your father knew that, and Peter knew that. He was not going to get away with what he'd done." Ray tried to explain, as Charlie shrugged off Ray's hand.

"Don't stand there and defend my father. He killed someone. If I consult for a company and they don't pay me, I don't kill them-or sorry, 'have' them killed. Okay, let me get this straight, and I know we have gone over this, but it just it not making sense. Peter owed my father $250,000. Peter paid him back $25,000 and wasn't going to pay back anything else, as far as you know. How do you know that this wasn't just the first installment of payments? Maybe he didn't have direct access to that much cash. Maybe $25,000 is all he had at that moment. I can't believe this Ray," Charlie said as he caught his breath. Visibly shaken, Charlie continued.

"So, because he only gave back $25,000, my father had him killed, or was aware of his killing. I'm having a very difficult time trying to believe this. I cannot believe I was so naïve, or stupid, or whatever. Fuck." Charlie turned his back on Ray and sat on the hood of the car. Ray could see his pounding heartbeat in the veins of his neck.

"Naive! You don't see it, do you? Peter was not an honest man. Maybe what we did to Peter wasn't the way you would have handled it, but it was the right thing to do. You weren't there; you cannot possibly understand." Ray was calm and collected, as if he was having a casual conversation with a friend.

"That can't be it. My father would not have killed someone, or had them killed, just because he didn't pay him back. There must be something else. Is there something you aren't telling me? If it was a matter of money, that just does not make sense. My father had enough money to last a lifetime, big deal 250k."

"No. That's it. You know everything Charlie. I know it is hard to imagine this kind of thing happening right now, in today's world, but try and put yourself in 1961. Times were much different; power and money were everything, they went hand in hand. If you had the money, then anything was possible. I think your dad was testing that theory. He was a powerful man. Your dad knew a lot of people, some very persuasive and powerful people. No one screwed with your dad, and he made that clear. Peter was the test, and your dad took that test. Don't you see, your dad wanted to test the boundaries, except he didn't have any boundaries, he was Aaron Rocklin. I'm not saying your dad was a bad person, or even a vindictive person, but I had never seen him like that before, that situation was different. On the other side, if word had gotten out that someone wronged your father in Vegas, someone else would have done the same thing. Your father was a protected man; he knew more than he should have about Vegas, the casinos and the owners. Your father didn't have a choice Charlie, you have to believe me on that."

"So, in 1961, Peter Rothwell was found dead. No one had any clues or leads? Come on, did he get the police on the payroll too?"

"Who said Peter was found in 1961?" Ray questioned.

Charlie began to blink uncontrollably. With a bewildered look on his face, he needed a few minutes.

"His-s-s-s body, was-s-s-s, never found?"

"Oh, no, it was found. But not in '61. That was 1965. Sure, there were a lot of people wondering and investigating into the disappearance of Peter Rothwell, but no one knew where to look or even where to start. Mary called the police and filed a missing person's report, but it was like trying to find Hoffa; where do you even begin? They looked and questioned some people, including your father, but nothing came of it. It was not until the 1965 murder trial of Jonathan "Meat" Rocco, when Peter Rothwell's name surfaced."

Charlie interrupted, "Wait, who is Rocco. Now we have someone named 'Rocco', Fuck me! This is starting to sound like a mafia movie."

"It is the mafia, my friend, and I was getting to that. Rocco was a known hit man for one of the Vegas families. He did favors for people. He was the guy you wanted to call and not one to call you. He was indicted on murder charges of a homeless man that was killed by the river. So, imagine Rocco, killing some trash like that. Now, everyone knew that Rocco did not waste his time on trash like that. He did the big jobs. He took out other family heads, big-time gamblers or police officers who weren't cooperating; not poor men who couldn't even afford to buy a loaf of bread. The feds had nothing else. They had been following Rocco for years and placed taps on every phone, car and hotel room he stayed in, but it never led to anything. Rocco was framed for this job. The trial went on for about six months and the prosecutor was getting buried. He did not have a case, but the Feds kept bringing in new evidence and the Judge never objected. Evidence was introduced that had nothing to do with the original indictment; that is when the family knew it was a setup, and so did Rocco.

Rocco had the best attorney money could buy.

His name was Anthony Beller and if he represented you,

you were somebody. You had to be important to get

Beller at your table. He had dis-credited all the

prosecuting witnesses. Made them contradict their own

story, questioning everything that came out of their

mouths. By the time he was done with cross-

examination, the witness' didn't even remember what

they said in the first place. Then when Rocco was on the

stand, he was brilliant. How many attorneys would put

their own client on the stand? Beller did. Rocco was in

Vegas when this poor guy was killed, the guy by the

river, but Rocco was nowhere near the river. He had an

alibi. The catch is, if he mentioned the alibi, then the

prosecutors would go after him, but that was the easiest

way for Beller to get the charges dropped. Rocco was

protecting the family and he did, but the alibi, who gave

a shit about him. At no time did Rocco want to be a snitch or call anyone out, but he was looking at life behind bars. If he could just reference this alibi and then talk to the family, he would clear his own name." Ray was out of breath.

March 15, 1965 - Murder Trial – One, Jonathan "Meat" Rocco, the accused.

Clark County Superior Court

Case number 65-00176

Beller: Your honor, I would like to call to the stand, Jonathan Rocco.

Judge: Counselor, you would like to call the defendant?

Beller: Yes, your honor.

Judge: Bailiff, please swear in the defendant.

Beller: Mr. Rocco, state your name and occupation for the record.

Rocco: My name is Jonathan Rocco and I own the 'Low Down Bar.'

Beller: What do you do at the bar Mr. Rocco?

Prosecution: Objection. This line of questioning is irrelevant to this case.

Beller: Your honor, I would like to establish the credit of my client. He is being indicted on murder charges, his credibility in this city is being questioned. I would like to show that Mr. Rocco is just like you or me. He is trying to make money to pay bills and support his family. He is a family man who attends church every Sunday. And the bar he owns is a means of making money. I will show that if I can continue with my line of questioning.

Judge: Objection over-ruled.

Beller: Mr. Rocco, What do you do at the bar?

Rocco: Well, I own it, so I do just 'bout everything there

is to do. I'm there to open the place in the morning and

to close the place every night. I handle all of the finances

of the bar and place all the orders for supplies. I serve

my customers. Hardworking men and women that

come in after a long day. I am always there. That what I

do.

Beller: How long have you owned this establishment?

Rocco: I would say 'bout five years now. I bought it

from this old guy who was goin' to retire. I wanted to

give him something to retire on. That is how I am. I'm

that kinda guy. A nice guy.

Beller: On January 17, 1965, a man came to the bar and

asked you some questions. Can you tell me about this?

Rocco: Yeah, A police officer came into the bar in early

evening and identified himself as officer, (slight pause)

oh, I cannot recall the name. Anyways, he was with the

Las Vegas Police Department. He said they found a

body down by the river on the east side. Now, I know

just as you do that there ain't no rivers in Vegas. You got

a go up to the mountains for that kind a thing, so right

then, at that moment, I knew some'in wasn't right. I

could smell me a rat.

Beller: Fine. Can you please get back to the questions

that the officer asked you?

Rocco: The officer asked where I was on the night of

December 24, 1964. I told him I was here, at the bar,

getting ready to close the place down for Christmas.

You know it was Christmas Eve, and on Christmas Eve, I

close early to be with my family. You know I have a

wife and t'ree kids. He asked if I could verify that. I said

to him, if you are asking me to proof to you that I am

married and have t'ree kids? He said, I bein' a smartass,

sorry your honor, but that's' just what he says to me.

No, you fuckin' wop, can you verify you were here, at

your bar, on Christmas Eve. So, I say, are you askin' me if there was anyone here in the bar on that evenin', I said sure, of course, but I don't knows' who. I see a lot of people in this place and it's impossible for me to recall everyone I talkin' to. I don't get names working here. I just give 'em what they want. Peoples come here to drink, your honor, it's a bar.

Beller: Did he ask you anything else?

Prosecution: Objection, leading the witness.

Judge: Sustained.

Beller: Was there another time that you were questioned?

Rocco: No. Not 'til these charges here.

Beller: So, there were no other police officers or detectives that came to ask questions about this man by the 'river'.

Rocco: No. No, not that I recall.

Beller: Okay fine, let's go back to the first time the officer came into the bar. In the report, it says that you could not recall any names of the patrons that evening.

Rocco: That is correct.

Beller: Are you telling me that there was no one in the bar that you knew by name. You must have regulars coming in and out of the bar. You stated, under oath, you owned this bar. Surely you can recall one name from a customer who is a regular at your bar.

Rocco: Sure, I have lots of regulars.

Beller: Can you recall any names from the night of December 24?

There was a long pause and a recess after this question. Rocco had a decision to make. In his line of business, you never gave another name. You never snitched on anyone because you would be ruined. The trust of the family would be questioned, and they would consider you a liability. And the family did not have liabilities. The decision to render a name would essentially get Rocco off the hook, as he would then have established an alibi. On the other hand, this would also expose Rocco as a not so trustworthy advisory, and he knew what happened to those who were considered not so trustworthy. He took care of these liabilities, he knew. The court was back in session.

Judge: Mr. Rocco, please remember you are still under oath.

Beller: Rocco, can you recall any names from the night of December 24, 1964, that were in the bar?

Rocco: There was this one guy sittin' at the bar. He was sittin' at the end. I do remember that.

Beller: Do you know the name of this person?

Rocco: He was a regular. I saw him least three times a week.

Beller: I want to ask you again Mr. Rocco, do you know the name of this person?

Rocco: I think his name was Jansen. (Looking at the judge) His name was Jansen.

Beller: Jansen. Was that his first or last name?

Rocco: I don't know. I just called him Jansen.

Beller: And this Jansen was in the bar on December 24, 1964. How can you be sure?

Rocco: How can I be sure? Because I know because I had invited him over for dinner as he was goin' be alone that evening. When he got there, he was feelin' pretty good. He continued to drink at the bar until all the other peoples had left. And that's when we began to talk.

Beller: Now, let me clear something up. You stated on the police report that you could not recall any names from that night. Why now are you telling this court about this Jansen character?

Rocco: Because I'm not a snitch. I do not rat on my friends. I believe in God and my family. They are first in my life. I can see that in order for me to put my family first, I have to tell you everything I know. If that means giving you a name, then I given' you a name. But I don't feel good about it, I'm not a snitch. This is not who I am. This is not right.

Beller: Mr. Rocco, I know this is hard for you, I really appreciate you being honest here, it is the right thing to do. That night, you said you and Jansen began to talk. What did you and Jansen talk about once every one left the bar?

Rocco: Mind you, hes' had a lot to drink. I mean he was well lit when he came in and he kept drinkin'. I mean, there was a time, when we doin' shots together. No one else was in da place, so we just drank.

Beller: I understand that fact. Please tell the court what you and Jansen discussed on the evening of December 24.

Rocco: Well, I remember closing up the bar. He kept just drinkin while I cleaned and closed the bar. Jansen and I sat at a table together and jus' started talking. He was telling me what a crazy night he had. He had been in a car accident that he can no longer drive his car, like totaled. I remember cause he says it was his girlfriend's car and he took it when she said 'no'. He was gonna be in deep shit, sorry your honor, excuse my French. And you know how a woman can get if you take somethin' without asking. I would not want to be in his shoes. Anyway, as he was walking out of a liquor store, he got mugged. The person took his wallet and all his money.

Prosecutor: Objection your honor, do we have to hear all this irrelevant information. Please instruct the defendant to answer the question. Your honor, please, what does this have to do with the charges before the defendant?

Judge: Mr. Prosecutor, is this your courtroom or mine? You do not tell me how to run my courtroom and I will not tell you how to prosecute this case. Mr. Rocco, is this story going somewhere?

Rocco: Yes, yours' honor. Please let me finish.

Judge: Objection overruled. You may continue Mr. Rocco.

Rocco: So, after he was robbed, he had nowheres' to go so he jus' startin' walkin'. He hitched a ride up the mountain and began to wonder down by the river and that is where he thought he saw the guy who robbed him. Jansen said he approached this guy and asked for his wallet and money back and the guy took a swing at him. Jansen then kicked him in the throat and pushed hims' in the water. The guy didn't move. He said he then begun to run and somehow ended up at my place.

Beller: So, let me get this straight, Jansen admitted to

you that he killed a guy by the river. Is this correct?

Rocco: Yeah, he said this guy did not move after he

pushed him. And then said that after the first time, it

did not feel as bad.

Beller: What did he mean 'after the first time."?

Prosecutor: Objection. What difference does it make?

That would be hearsay, and none the less irrelevant to

this case.

Beller: Your honor, I'm merely establishing the fact that

this Jansen character is a repeat offender. I would like

the court to know the background of Jansen as a fact that

he is capable of such a crime and that my client is

unjustly indicted and being accused of this crime.

Judge: Objection overruled. Mr. Rocco, please continue.

Rocco: After a couple more drinks he said that that was

not the first time he had killed a man. He said that he

killed a man a few years ago as a favor to a friend and at

the time and he was nervous. But this bein' the second

time and all, or maybe third or fourth time, he did not

feel as bad. I think he was a little too drunk if you know

what I mean, he was talkin' crazy, but I kinda of believe

him, at the time, I mean, who was I to question him? I

didn't want to get his mad at me, considering he just told

me that he killed someone. I have a family and t'ree

kids, I don't need that in my life.

Beller: No further questions for my client. After hearing

the immediate testimony of my client, I would like the

charges of murder be dropped and my client to be set

free.

No judge in their right mind would let a person

go free, based on their own testimony, admittingly

drunk, without any other evidence, especially a person

like Meat. Vegas knew who Meat was, they all knew

what this guy did for a living, and it was not serving

drinks to degenerates. The judge stayed the proceedings

to further investigate Jansen's story of the man being

kicked in the throat and the possible murder of a guy a

few years ago. It took several months to track down this

person, Jansen, while Rocco waited in a jail cell. But

once they did, Jansen sang like a bird. Thanks to Rocco,

Jansen was questioned and within an hour of being

questioned, he had confessed to both murders and led

the police to the scene of the other murder. It was deep

in the Vegas desert. The sun was beating down and

temperatures reached 115 degrees. The exact location

was not known, but after several weeks of digging and

probing by the police and federal agents, the body of

Peter Rothwell was found buried ten feet below the hot

desert earth.

"So, they found the body, thanks to Rocco. Now

that Jansen was arrested and charged, didn't he tell the police the truth?" Charlie asked.

"No, not Jansen. It was his fault that he got too drunk in the first place. That was his weakness. Once he confessed, he knew he was alone. He also knew that if he had said a word, his life would be over and that no one would be able to protect him, no matter where he was. You did not want to have the family against you. So Jansen said what he needed to say and that was that. He was done, he knew he was done, and he took it like a man. Unfortunately for Jansen, he was killed one night in his cell. Someone slit his throat from ear to ear." Ray said

"Jesus fucking Christ, Ray! This is totally crazy. Seriously, I cannot believe what you are telling me. And then what about Peter's wife? What did she do after all this time?"

"Mary was the one who started all this in the first place. Because her and Peter gave a ton of money to the Police Department Charity drives and a bunch of other shit, they felt a little obligated to keep the case opened until solved."

"But it was solved. Jansen confessed to the killing."

"Not so fast. The crime was solved, but that did not satisfy Mary. She asked that the case remain open for further investigation. Even though there were no leads of any kind, and on paper it was a closed case, it remained open. The police questioned your father one last time after the arrest, and then never bothered him again. Mary was still not satisfied, she always felt like there was someone else involved besides Jansen. Mary wanted the case open because she thought she knew the truth, but no one would listen. No one would go against your father and the people he knew. Aaron was a very well-known and respected man in Vegas. The Rothwells may have given generously to the police, but they knew the connections your father had, and no one would touch that. But as a courtesy to Mary, and to keep her generosity coming, they left the case open."

Charlie sat there running his hands through his hair, pulling out strands, still in disbelief. Just as when he heard this the first time in Tahoe, he still could not believe that his parents could have done something so vile, so wrong, against everything he was taught.

"So why did this all come about now, some thirty years later?" Charlie asked.

"Like I said, a detective Tricks came to see me here in Florida because Mary had passed away. Tricks wanted one last time to finally close the case, just ask a few more questions. He felt that it was the least he could do, in her memory. I mean, they had kept this thing

open all these years just because she was still alive."

"That's right, she died. Wow. This is unreal. So,

Tricks was just closing the case with you because you

knew my parents? And no one else knows about this?"

"No one but you and me, kid, and that is where

this should stay. Between you and me. Your parents are

gone, Peter is gone, and now Mary is gone. There is no

one else,"

"Ok, I think I understand now, but one question

Ray. Why are you telling me this? Everyone is gone and

if no one else knows, why bring it up? This could have

died with you and honestly, I would have been alright

with that."

"I thought about that, and I was holding on to

this for a while, debating whether or not to even say

anything. The more I played it out in my head, I just felt

like you should know. If anything, ever came out, ever, I

didn't want you to hear it from someone else or second

hand. I wanted you to hear it directly from me," Ray

concluded.

Chapter Eight

In an incoherent daze, Charlie walked up the stairs to his plane, holding on to the rails, his mind swirling with the inconceivable information Ray had thrown at him. He'd just heard extremely disturbing news about his parents, and most disturbing, about his own father. This was a man who use to kiss Charlie every night before he went to bed; a man who would tuck him in at night and read him bedtime stories. A man who would even attend church, occasionally. But here was a man, a husband and a father, who committed the worst of all crimes. Charlie's father, a murderer. A man took another man's life, just because he could. A man who thought power could bring him everything, and apparently it did.

Charlie walked through the door to his plane. As soon as the door closed, all of that was gone, out of his mind. No matter what Ray said, all Charlie wanted to do was get home to Serina. Charlie walked by Alice, his flight attendant, said "hello" and took his seat.

Sitting in his executive lounge chair in the middle of the plane, Charlie closed his eyes. Before the plane even began to taxi, Charlie reclined his chair and felt at peace, picturing Serina in his arms, by his side. He missed that beautiful face, he missed her touch, and he missed being around her, all the time. Charlie wanted desperately to forget what he just heard, but he could not get it out of his head. He opened his eyes and tried to focus on Serina, but it didn't work. Memories of his father kept crowding his mind with images of a towering figure standing over a dead body. Unable to relax, Charlie began to pace the aisle of the plane.

With a cruising altitude of 30,000 feet, Charlie

picked up the phone to talk to Serina. Charlie was

exhausted. This had been a long and emotional day, but

he wanted nothing more than to forget what he just

heard and be with his newfound obsession. All he

wanted to do was distract himself, and Serina was just

the distraction he needed. Charlie's plane had 10

executive lounge chairs, 5 on each side of the plane with

an automatic retracting coffee table in the middle. The

coffee table would come up when the plane reached 10

thousand feet. There was a small room for the attendant

and supplies before a door leading to the master

bedroom. The bedroom had a king size bed with a

sitting area that was accompanied by two chairs and a

small table. Charlie was too exhausted to even make it

to the bedroom.

Serina picked up the phone, "Hello my beautiful,

how was your day?" Charlie asked in an exhausted

voice, but with a smile.

"Honestly, it was a little lonely here. I really miss

when you are not here. Please tell me you are on your

way. Where did your work take you this time?" Serina

asked.

"I am in flight and should land in about four

hours, just took off from Miami. But I am not coming

home to you. I am coming home for you."

"What in the world were you doing in Miami?"

Serina probed.

"Just a little business and visiting an old friend.

But what is important is me coming home for you, not to

you!"

"Does that not mean the same thing Charlie?"

"No beautiful, it means that when I get home, I

will be waiting in the car, I don't even want to walk into

that place. I want you to come out and I want to take

you away. I need to be with you, right now, tonight. So,

whatever you have planned for the next three days,

cancel them, you will be busy. See you in a few hours."

Charlie hung up the phone and closed his eyes for the

rest of the flight.

Something happened during that short trip to

Miami, and it was the exact opposite of what Ray had

intended. Rather than planting a seed of caution and

skepticism, Charlie came to the conclusion that he did

not want to be alone. He did not want to spend his days

traveling, meeting with people, and missing out on the

things in life that made him smile. He did not want to

turn into his parents. Charlie had needed to hear the

story directly from Ray, but Charlie didn't seem to care.

He actually did care, but he was not able to see the forest

through the trees. He was not able, or he did not want to

connect the dots. Charlie was there, he was present, but was he really listening to what Ray was saying? Ray did not know exactly what or who Serina was, but all he could do was tell Charlie the truth and hoped it would all shake out from there. Of course, Charlie cared about what Ray was telling him, but never before had Charlie been able to share his life with someone other than his assistant. Never before had Charlie felt so comfortable with someone.

Whether it was the news of his parents or the fact that Charlie wanted to begin to enjoy what he had worked so hard for, he needed to get away. He needed to think and be with someone who made him feel good about himself, because at this moment, he was lost. Everything he thought he knew about his parents; he began to question. He was not giving up on everything he'd worked for; he just needed some time. And who else to spend this time with than one person he felt closest to? The one thing Ray didn't tell Charlie was his concern with Serina. Although Ray didn't know this woman, he did have a gut feeling that something was not right.

Charlie landed at the Lake Tahoe airport. Waiting on the tarmac was a limousine. They headed straight for home. Just as he instructed, Serina was ready and waiting on the doorstep, sitting outside, looking great under the moonlit sky. Charlie got out of the limo and walked toward Serina. Without saying a word, he picked her up and kissed her. Before turning around and heading back to the limo, Charlie carried her inside the house, and laid her on the marble floor under the great chandelier that illuminated the spiral staircase. He kissed her lips and neck and caressed her as if he had been away for months. His hands moved up and down, covering every part of her tanned body. Removing her dress strap with his mouth, he slipped the dress down to her feet and it fell to the floor. Charlie stood up and removed his clothes. He started at the bottom, kissing her toes, moving up to her legs and then her inner thigh, as she trembled with pleasure. His tongue led the way between her legs, he could feel Serina's back arch up. Charlie had never been so hard, he needed to feel her, be inside of her. He crawled on top of her and kissed her lips, down to the back of her neck and felt himself slide inside of her. She let out a moan, opened her eyes to see his watery, emotion-filled eyes, and then closed hers. As Charlie was enjoying what he came home for, Serina, eyes still closed, smiled.

Walking out of the house and into the limo, Serina asked where they were going, but Charlie would not let the secret out. All she knew was that she will be returning on Sunday night. She kept asking, but to no avail. As the limo drove past the airport, Serina was left wondering. Heading down the highway, Charlie told her it will be a couple hours until they arrived at their first stop. Serina took off her shoes, and put her head on Charlie's lap, her eyes closing quickly.

Although the moment could not be more perfect, Charlie stared out the window, watching the stars above. He began to replay the news about his father in his head. How could a man that was such a great husband and father have such a dark side? How many times did this other side appear? Was there more that Charlie didn't know? Sometimes there are things that you don't need to know, things that you would be better off not knowing. But Charlie knew, and he was growing more curious with each passing white line on the road. His eyes eventually grew heavy and closed.

The limo pulled up to a little house near the end of the Napa Valley in a town called Calistoga. Charlie went to Calistoga five years ago for business. Thinking he would visit more often; he had purchased a bed and breakfast. This was the first time in those five years that he'd returned. Doris had called the caretaker when Charlie was still in Florida and arranged for the four-bedroom house to be theirs for the weekend. It was a charming little place, settled on just under an acre of land. A rather large plot of land if you weren't a winery.

Serina lifted her head to look around and asked if they had arrived. It was dark except for the lighted, winding pathway leading to the front door. Charlie took his hand, raised her head, and kissed her on the lips. "We are here," he said. There is a slight chill in the air with the smell of smoke from a wood burning fire. Hearing the flowing water from the fountains in the back of the house, Charlie took Serina's hand and led her to

the front door that was concealed with the massive

valley oaks that surround the entrance. Music can be

heard from the porch as they made their way to the

door.

The door is opened with a push of a button from

the kitchen, into a waiting area with benches on each

side, burning candles that hung on the wall and entrance

to the main house. He smiled, knowing they are only a

few miles from home, but felt like thousands. Charlie

led Serina through the second doorway that opened up

to a 30-foot, castle-like foyer, surrounded by rectangular,

misplaced windows near the top. As he walks her

inside, they are greeted by Minnie, the caretaker.

Minnie, you could say, came with the property when

Charlie purchased it. She had been there for 25 years; it

was something her and her husband started. When

Minnie's husband passed away from Melanoma in 2000, Minnie wanted to do nothing else but keep his memory alive by continuing to be part of the property.

Minnie took their coats and led them to the dining room, where the candlelit table was set for two. Wine is chilling on the side table, and the soup is steaming as it is placed before the two guests. Serina sits and Charlie sits next. He raises his glass and toasts to his love for Serina and how good she makes him feel. Before he can take the first sip, Serina toasts to her love as well.

"Charlie, you make me the happiest woman on Earth. I couldn't have ever imagined that I would have met someone like you, who treats me so well. I love you." Serina said with her glass raised. With a tilt of her head and a sultry wink, they drink.

Dinner is a seven-course meal with several

palette cleansers between the different courses. From the dining room table, the fire in the living room is burning and glowing off Serina's face. You can hear the crackle with fresh burning pine scent filling air. Charlie was madly in love with this girl, whom he did not know very well.

Starting off with shrimp cocktail and raw oysters, the staff begins to fill the table with a variety of appetizers to choose from. A fresh mixed green salad will follow and then a small bowl of lime sorbet to prepare the senses for the main course(s). A butterflied fillet served on a bed of wild rice with a burgundy mushroom sauce with fresh vegetables around the rice, sprinkled with paprika. Just when Serina thought she was complete, the seventh and final course was served. A flaming soufflé' filled with bananas foster. Prepared tableside, and flamed with brandy, Charlie got up and prepared this himself.

After the dessert was taken in, a side of Henri IV Dudognon Heritage Cognac was poured from the world's most expensive bottle of cognac.

Minnie led Charlie and Serina to their room upstairs. Their robes were laid on the bed, and they were instructed to put them on for their full body massages and body wraps from the licensed masseuse. The treatments were done in the room and Charlie and Serina went to bed immediately afterward, another word was not spoken.

In the morning, they were greeted by the fresh smell of brewing coffee and breakfast being cooked. Charlie turned his head to Serina and kissed her forehead.

"What do you think of Calistoga so far?" Charlie asked.

"I love this place. I could stay here forever lying in your arms. It is just as relaxing as I remember." Serina said as she closed her sleepy eyes.

"As you remember?" Charlie asked. "So, you've been here before?"

She opened her eyes as if she'd been rudely awakened. "Yes. I haven't been to this particular place, but I went to Napa with my parents a long time ago. We took a trip up here to get out of Vegas."

"I've never heard you speak of your parents before. Do you talk to them much?"

"No, they both passed away."

"Did you say Las Vegas?"

"Yes, we lived in Las Vegas."

"Oh, I'm sorry. I had no idea. You never said anything before. Forgive me for bringing it up."

"It's not a problem, don't worry about it. So,

what are we going to do today?"

Charlie sat up and propped a pillow up behind his back.

"Wait a minute. Tell me a little more about your parents. What are their names, what did your parents do? How did they pass?"

"What did you say Charlie?" Serina asked in a defensive tone, one that Charlie had not heard before.

"I um, I'm just asking about your parents, what are their names and what did your parents do in Las Vegas?"

"What is this fascination with my parents all of a sudden? I mention them once and you start in with the twenty questions. Can you please just drop my parents. There're both dead, and I'd rather not talk about it."

Puzzled Charlie turned his head and nodded. Of course, it is not a pleasant conversation to discuss the loss of your parents and one may even get uncomfortable, but to truly get to know someone, you would want to know where they came from, who they came from. For the first time, Charlie began to wonder about his girlfriend. Serina laid in silence for about ten minutes and got out of bed to look out the window. The sun was shining off her nude body as the blinds were opened. Charlie turned to face the light and stared at Serina's perfect figure that was glowing. She turned around with that smile Charlie could not resist, and said "I love you; you know that right?"

"I know that."

Charlie got out of bed and walked toward Serina. He put his arms around her and spoke softly in her ear, "You know you can talk to me about anything. What you are feeling, why you are feeling that way. I'm here for you, now and forever. I do want to get to know you, and the real you, and that means getting to know where you came from, your family. I will be here whenever you are ready."

Charlie rubbed her bare back and worked his way down. Serina was still staring out the window, lips slightly pursed, eyes half closed and squinted, as if she was contemplating what to say or do next. Charlie put his hands on her shoulders and turned her around to face him. He kissed her lips and kissed her forehead. If there was anything in the world that would change the subject, this would be it. Serina kissed him back, brought her hands to his mid-section and squeezed his ass. He lifted her up, and brought her to the shower and carried her inside. The water was cold at first, but they barely noticed. Serina was sitting on the little bench that was built into the shower toward the back. As the water began to get hotter, the steam sauna kicked on, screaming hot water from the little metal spigot by their feet. Serina began to vocalize her pleasure as Charlie was on his knees, between her legs. He raised his head and kissed her stomach and worked his way up to her lips, where he touched them and kissed them all over, taking small gentle bites of her bottom lip.

The water was hitting Charlie in the back as he had Serina pushed up against the glass shower door, perfectly pressing against to outline her body. Kissing her neck and raising one leg to the bench, Charlie inserted himself. Moving slow at first and getting more aggressive, Charlie could feel it all coming to an end. Serina pushed him away, turned herself around, and bent over to place her hands on the middle of the glass. Reaching around, she helped Charlie back inside. Just as Charlie was reaching his limit, Serina began to smile. Just before Charlie released himself, he glanced through the steam and could see Serina's face in the glass. Seeing her half-devious smile, he began to look around; he could sense something, but it was too late. Charlie came inside, hard. He rested on her back while he caught his breath. Serina lifted her head and turned to look into his eyes.

"I have been waiting for a long, long time for you. I have been in search of you. I will never let you go."

"Never?" he said.

"Not ever. I, we have so much to do yet."

After the shower, a ringing of a bell indicated that breakfast was ready. Charlie and Serina finished getting dressed and headed down the stairs, where they were greeted by Minnie.

"How was your sleep?" she inquired.

"Wonderful. We had a great night, thanks for setting it all up." Charlie said, sounding more relaxed than he had ever been.

After a light breakfast, they were off to tour some of the wineries.

"What does our day have in store for us?" Serina asked, knowing most likely what the answer was going to be.

"Wouldn't you like to know!"

Heading toward the door, Serina could see the shadow of a car through the center glass in the front door. Awaiting them was their Calistoga "Uber", Charlie's deep metallic blue Aston Martin DBX. The plan was four private tours, ending at a small Pinot winery, Failla. Charlie stumbled upon Failla winery several years back. Lost and looking to turn around, he saw the little sign covered by overgrown foliage. Walking up to the little tasting house, he noticed the winemaker turning the "open" sign to "closed".

Mentioning that he had never heard of the brand before, the winemaker opened up the door and gave Charlie a private tour of the vineyard and sampling of their latest vintage. Before Charlie left, he purchased 10 cases and joined their wine club.

It was the perfect place to end their day. The courtyard was decorated with hanging lights, with one table on the cobblestone patio that was illuminated by two candles. Dinner for two was served by a host of waiters. During the course of two hours, Charlie and Serina had devoured every morsel of food and three bottles of their Occidental Ridge Pinot. The evening concluded with a tour of the Failla cave, and two cases of their most recent vintage of Pinot's. Escorted out, Charlie takes Serina's hand and opens the rear door to the Aston. With a grin, Serina noticed her purse was sitting in the back seat. She had left it back at the

Calistoga house, knowing they would return later that evening, she was wrong.

"What is this doing here? I didn't bring that."

"That was only the first night my dear," Charlie said with a kiss, closing the door.

The sun was setting on the hills of the Napa Valley, as they headed north, to the Oregon Coast. Stopping outside of a gated residence, the ten-foot metal gates opened slowly to reveal a modest little, single story 7000-square-foot house, 50 feet from the waves of the Pacific Ocean. The sound of the ocean echoed in the air as if there was a conch shell being held by your ear. When the waves receded, getting ready to make their way back, there was utter silence. Stars illuminated the pathway to the house. Charlie and Serina made their way down the pathway, looking up at the heavens.

The butler greeted them kindly and showed them

to their room. Their room was the entire west wing of the house. Upon entering the master, you are immediately reminded of the privileged life Charlie led. You entered a sitting room with a fireplace that opened up to an office with custom built in credenza and desk. The walls were lined with autographs from some of Charlie's clients. The heated floors were solid marble that led to the master bed and a gigantic marble double-sided fireplace. The balcony wrapped around the entire floor with an outdoor fireplace that was filling the air with the smell of freshly burning oak. Once their luggage was brought up from the car, Charlie placed a new black Giorgio Armani crystal-embellished dress on the bed.

"I want you to wear this tonight. I want you to look even more beautiful, if that is even possible. I want everyone to be looking at you!" Charlie said as he removed his travel clothes and pulled out a garment bag

with a tuxedo inside.

Getting back into the car, Charlie handed Serina a

dozen long-stemmed roses, followed by a kiss on the

cheek.

"You look absolutely beautiful this evening. Care

to join me?" Charlie said with a smirk. A smile was his

answer.

The restaurant was Hilltop Manor. It was an old

1800's mansion that was completely renovated for the

purpose of a restaurant. Each table has its own

dedicated server, a waiter, a runner and a bus boy. The

tables are set with embossed napkins of your initials and

each person at the table has a book of matches, printed

with your name, table number and date of your dining

experience. The napkins and matches are yours to keep,

but everything else stays. Their dinner reservations

were at 6:00, and Charlie and Serina didn't leave until 11:15, which was expected considering the dining experience.

Exiting the restaurant, the air was brisk. You could feel the chill coming in off the ocean and hear the high tide waves crashing into the rocks. The driver was waiting to take Charlie and Serina back to the house. During the short ride, Serina cuddled up next to Charlie as he buried his nose in the smell of her hair. It was just after midnight by the time they made it back to the house. Candles were burning, the bed was turned down, the Jacuzzi was foaming, and the pool was warmed to 78 degrees. Charlie took off his clothes and went for a swim, and Serina sat naked, with her feet in, at the end of the pool, watching him. Charlie did a few laps, swam up next to Serina, and pulled her in.

Taking her to a place in the pool where only he

could stand, Charlie held Serina close to his body.

"I could not stand to just look at you any longer sitting up there. You looked fucking amazing."

"What is all this? Why are you doing this, Charlie?"

"What is all this? Why am I doing all this? There are a few reasons. Because I love you, because I can, and because of you. There are no limits with me. I will go to any lengths for you, at any cost. The first time I laid eyes on you, I knew. I had the feeling, the same feeling even now when I look at you. A feeling that I have never felt before. One that touched my heart, and one that I want to keep in my heart. You are the most beautiful thing I have ever seen. Your hair, your lips, your smile, your taste and your touch. I love you. And that is why I'm doing all this. I am doing this all for you."

"And what is so special about me? You can have

any woman you want."

"There is something about you. Maybe it's the way you talk to me, as if you have nothing to lose. You may like what you see around you, but honestly, I don't see that side of you. You could take this or leave it. Everyone I meet, they see me only for what I have and not for what I am. To me, you are different like that. Am I wrong?"

"No, you aren't wrong. I do like all this, I like what you give me, and I like what you can give me, but that is not why I'm with you."

"Then why are you with me?" he asked.

Serina just smiled and said nothing. She leaned in to kiss Charlie. The conversation was over, and they continued in the bedroom.

The next morning came a knock at the door. "Mr. Rocklin, this is your 8:30 wake up call," came a voice on the other side of the door.

"I took the liberty and ordered you a massage and facial. I need to make a few calls to the office and will be back in about two hours. Is that alright with you?" Charlie asked.

"Of course. Who am I to say no to a massage and facial? Now go, make those calls." Serina said as she touched his face and kissed his lips.

Charlie called Doris to check in and get his messages - forty-two in the past twenty-four hours. Most of them were from existing clients needing to ask questions or seek business advise; nothing that can't wait until Monday, just one more day. But there was a call from Ray. Not just one, or two, but five calls. Doris said he sounded kind of worried, as he had never known Charlie to just drop everything and go out of town for days on end. This was not the Charlie that Ray or anyone else was used to, Ray was concerned. Ray would not say what he wanted; only that he wanted Charlie to call him back as soon as possible. Charlie was still numb from the recent news about his father, but Ray was a friend, and good friends are hard to come by. Charlie's next call was to Ray.

"Ray, what's going on? You call me five times in 24 hours. I can only assume you are still alive if I'm talking to you, so what seems to be the problem?"

"Glad you called me back. I have known you your entire life, and not once have I ever known you to just pick up and leave, during a work week no less. What the fuck is going on with you man? Please tell me that this is not your new thing. Please tell me this is not all for that chick."

"First of all, I have gone out of town several times before now. Second, this is about Serina. She's the most beautiful thing in the world. I never thought I could ever love someone this much, but I've been proven wrong. You will meet her soon, I promise. I know you have seen her, but next time, I will properly introduce you two. She is truly one of a kind."

"Listen here, I've said it before, you need to watch yourself. Whoever this girl is, I mean who she really is, you don't know her. I wish I could tell you something differently, but I will look into your Serina. You have a lot to offer a young woman, maybe too much. Sometimes money can be a bad thing, so for fuck sake man, just be careful and keep your eyes open. This Serina, what is she like, what does she do?" Ray asked.

"She is great. She, you know, I really don't have an idea what she does. All I know is that she's always there when I need her to be. She stays at my place, so I don't even know where she lives. Not that I have thought about this before, but I never really gave it much thought. I know we like the same things, or at least I think we do. Ray, you just have to meet her."

"I have, remember, at Frankie's place. She's the one who knocked on the door in the early hours of the morning, and that was enough meeting for me. She is the one you ran off with that night. I know if she is with you, she must be something pretty special. Well, I'd best be going. I just wanted to make sure you were alright. To be honest, I am a little concerned, I'm worried about you. Take care of yourself and learn more about your mysterious Serina. I'm sure there is a story behind her and I'm going to do some digging." Ray hung up the phone knowing Charlie was not about to dive into anything else he had to say.

Charlie did not want to think about what he *should* be thinking about. He did not want to ask questions and for that matter, he did not need to know the answers. In his job, he was in control, he was the one holding the cards. Every minute of every day, Charlie had to think. He had to be on 100% of the time, and that was exhausting. This was not that kind of relationship. It was so opposite than what Charlie had to deal with every day, and he kind of liked not knowing, letting go. Not so much in control. But what happens when you are not in control, you often lose control. He tried to tell himself he did not care or want to know, but it was eating him up inside. When he thought about broaching the subject of her past, with Serina, he recalled the way she'd acted about her parents the other night. Charlie enjoyed the change, the release of control; but now was not the time to shake things up.

Charlie returned a few other calls and told Doris to set up some meetings upon his return on Monday. By

10:00 a.m., Charlie made his way back to the room while he was finishing up on a call. The door to the suite closed, and Serina appeared from the back bedroom wearing a very short white-lace silk, see-through robe. A distracted Charlie was no longer listening to whoever was on the other end of the phone. His eyes were glued on Serina as she slowly pranced across the room, getting his undivided attention. Her robe falls off her shoulders and onto the floor. The phone still up to his ear, Charlie watches intently as she heads toward the sauna. Without saying goodbye, he ends the call, follows Serina into the bathroom, shedding his clothes as he approaches.

A plume of thick steam fills the air as Serina opens the sauna door. The temperature gauge on the wall read 140 degrees. Serina turns the temperature up to 180, turns around and gives Charlie a look before entering. Charlie follows closely behind and closes the

door behind him. Serina turns him around and rubs his

body from behind, starting at his ears, down to his neck,

and reaching her hands around to his chest. Charlie

disappeared in the thick steam that was overtaking the

sauna. She kneels down behind him and kisses his legs

and backside while her hands are in motion elsewhere.

Still on her knees, unable to see, she uses her hands to

turn Charlie around and puts himself in her mouth.

Charlie braces himself with his hands on the wet walls

dripping with humidity. Not wanting it to end this way,

Charlie pulls Serina up and sits on the cut-out bench in

the corner of the shower, sweat pouring off his body. He

grabs Serina, sits her down on his lap and watches

himself slide in and out of her. Wiping his forehead, he

reaches around and cups her breasts in his hands, feeling

her hard nipples. Thrusting in and out, kissing the back

of her neck, Charlie does not have his usual stamina. He apologizes for his abruptness, and Serina puts her finger to his mouth and enjoys the moment.

Sitting on the bench and both breathing heavy from the activity, Charlie notices the temperature gauge: 195. Needing to cool down, Serina glances at the pool.

"Let's go for a swim," she says.

"I'm sorry this weekend has to end," Charlie commented as Serina swam around him.

"This has been the greatest time of my life. You've made a great life for yourself, Charlie. You live very well, and I could not be happier to be the one you are sharing it with. But this weekend must end, so we can have others. We have only just begun to enjoy our time together."

Calling for the car to get ready for the journey home, Charlie and Serina packed up and left Oregon.

When they arrived home that evening, they headed

straight for bed. They did not wake up until Doris called

at 6 am on Monday morning, making sure Charlie was

up for his busy day and ready for the week ahead.

Chapter Nine

"Good morning Mr. Rocklin. A very busy day and week ahead, we have a lot of catching up to do." Doris greeted Charlie as he arrived on Monday morning at 7:30.

Doris went into her normal speech reviewing Charlie's calendar to map out the day and notifying Charlie of what and where he was headed. After going over the phone messages, Doris began.

"You have Paul at 9:30, he will be your first appointment. I did not want to start you off too early having just come back. At 10:00, at the Hyatt, Bill Patterson will meet you out on the balcony, he has wired you $250,000 for last quarter, and would like to clarify the reminder of this year and start their FY21 planning.

You are having lunch today with Frankie also at the Hyatt; he will be there at 11:00. At 1:00, here at the office, you will need to sign some papers from the mayor about the library that you are funding. He wants to get a brief bio and ask some questions. I can screen them if you'd like. There will be a dedication at the library, and he will give you some dates. I'll be in the meeting with your calendar. At 2:15, Roger Ricker wants to drop off a retainer for the Xerox Corporation and would like to set up a meeting sometime early next month with the board. He's in town with family, so he said he would just stop in. And finally, at 3:30, you need to meet Rand at his office to discuss your investments for the month. He has made some recommendations to your proposal and has not heard back from you. Later tonight at 10:00 pm, you have a conference call with Japan and speak to Jon Yen and three of their board members. It will be 3:00 pm tomorrow there."

A light day for Charlie, considering what his normal daily routine was. Doris could tell he was not all there when she was speaking. She had made the right choice to lighten his first day back. She was growing concerned about the business, but most importantly concerned about Charlie. She may not have all the details, but when Ray was calling non-stop and Charlie was a disappearing act, her gut told her something is wrong. Doris was getting very close to asking Charlie what was going on, but decided to hold off until he got settled back in to work.

Sitting at his desk and glancing at his watch, the time was 9:15. Charlie picked up his phone and dialed the house.

"Rocklin residence," Brian answered.

"Brian, how are you?"

"I'm well, and you?"

"Doing well. Listen, is Serina there?"

"She hasn't come down from the room yet. Would you like me to ring her for you?"

"No, no. That's alright. Just have her call when she appears."

Charlie had just finished with his 9:30 and as he was walking to his car to drive to the Hyatt to meet Mr. Paterson, he glanced once more at his watch. The time was 9:50, and still no call from Serina.

"Rocklin residence," Brian answered.

"Brian, it's me again. Sorry to keep calling, but I need to speak to Serina. Can you please ring her for me?"

"Ring her for you?"

"Yes, can you please get Serina on the phone."

"Sorry for not knowing, but how exactly would

you like me to do that?" Brian asked in a slow but unknown tone.

"Can you please walk up the stairs and tell Serina I am on the phone."

"Didn't she ring you?"

"Ring me? No, she did not. Is there a problem?"

"Mr. Rocklin, Serina is not here."

Charlie immediately pulled over to the side of the road. He hung up the phone and looked at the calmness of the lake and the reflections of the mountains. As if his heart jumped out of the car, he turned around and headed for home. Waiting for the gates to open, Brian came out of the house and stood on the front porch. Before the car came to a complete stop, Charlie opened his door.

"She came down just after we spoke the first time, and I informed her to call you. She then went back upstairs for a few minutes and then left. She walked right past me, she did not say a word. When I asked her when she would be back, she just looked at me and smiled."

"What are you talking about, who are you talking about?" Charlie asked, knowing exactly who Brian was talking about.

"Serina. She has left. Her Uber came about an hour ago."

With his car still running and without closing his driver side door, Charlie walked inside the house. He pulled his phone out of his jacket pocket and went to dial Serina. Except there was one problem: he did not have a number for her. It had almost been six months, and he'd never gotten her last name or phone number. Mostly due to the fact that Serina was always around Charie or at the house, it wasn't a priority at the time, but that is about to change.

Charlie ran upstairs, looking around the house as he passed other rooms. Making his way into the bedroom, he noticed nothing of Serina's. When he got to the master closet, he saw that some of her stuff was still hanging in the bathroom and on her side of the closet. He found it hard to believe that Serina would just pack up and leave. Charlie sat on the bed, scratching his head. Unable to comprehend what was happening, Charlie looked at his watch. He was late for lunch with Frankie. Quickly pulling himself together as best he could, he walked down the stairs.

"Brian, I'm heading to meet Frankie at the Hyatt. If Serina returns, can you please call me?"

"Will do!"

Charlie got into his car and headed off to meet Frankie.

Lunch with Frankie

Charlie was not his usual self at lunch. He barely spoke a word, and Frankie could see Charlie was hurting. When you know someone as long as Frankie knew Charlie, he did not have to say that anything was wrong. Frankie knew it, and he was not afraid to ask.

"Charlie, you have known this girl for less than six months. What were you thinking not getting her last name or even her phone number? I don't understand what you have been doing with this girl man. This is so not like you, in every way, that I know you. Dude, what do you really know about Serina, other than her first name?" Charlie sat there looking through Frankie.

And deep inside, he began to think about what he was doing.

Seeing his eyes tear up, Frankie tried again with a

little more compassion.

"Listen, C, maybe things were moving a little too fast for her. Maybe she needed some time to think. You have a lot to offer, and it can be a little overwhelming. Maybe you were coming on a little too strong? Or maybe, she's doing you a favor." Frankie tried to make Charlie feel better, but to no avail.

The circumstances were indeed a little strange. As Charlie gave Frankie a detailed description of their weekend together, the puzzle just didn't fit together. How often do two people have a wonderful, perfect weekend, and then one of them disappears without reason? Unless something happened to Serina. But Brian said he saw her get into a car and drive off. She'd left and dealing with it was the hardest part for Charlie. As Charlie began to replay everything in his mind, this was not the first time he'd felt like this. He would talk to

Frankie about the weekend, then replay that back in his mind, over and over again. It was as if there was a tiny tape recorder, hitting play, then rewind. Play, then rewind. But the end result was still the same: she was gone.

After hearing the details, Frankie became concerned. Frankie could tell that Charlie really liked this woman. This was the first time Frankie could recall Charlie being so enamored with someone. There have been other girls before, but not like this, not someone who made Charlie break character. Frankie decided to try a different approach. He began to ask about their relationship. He asked about Serina; what she did during the day, what they did at night, and how they met. Charlie answered the questions with brief sentences while staring off into the distance, without making eye contact with Frankie. He then asked Charlie

what he knew about Serina. There was silence. Frankie
wasn't concerned about the whereabouts or safety of
Serina, but he expressed deep concern for Charlie.
Something wasn't right, and Frankie knew it. Everyone
fucking knew it, but Frankie said it.

"You know what, maybe you should call
someone who can check into this girl. I am willing to bet
that Ray can find something on her? I mean you need to
protect yourself. This girl seems 'too good to be true'
and too weird to be anything else. She appears out of
nowhere, she noticed you! And she made sure you
noticed her. She knew what cars you drive even before
she knew you. She knew where you worked, where you
ate, and you still don't even know her last name? It is
not like you, to not ask those questions. To me, it sounds
like it was a predisposed plan, premeditated Charlie.
Are you listening to me? She isn't who you think she is,

man; she is the fucking devil. Are you going to call Ray, or should I?"

"You're right, and I should have done this long ago. I should have listened to Ray; I will call him." Charlie said slowly, looking at Frankie.

"He can do a background check and help fill in the missing pieces. Yeah, I do think I might want to look into that. You know what, these past few months are a blur. I have been so preoccupied with Serina, I don't even remember what I'm doing at the office. I cannot recall phone calls; I don't have the desire to talk to anyone and I really don't care. All I think about is Serina. Maybe I need to be grounded. Maybe this is a wakeup call. Shit, I don't know what the fuck is going on. What I can tell you is that I am done with this. I felt so happy, yet I feel so lost with everything else in my world."

Frankie seemed to have broken through the wall. This was the first time Charlie was able to listen to what someone else had to say about Serina. Frankie gave Charlie the motivation to take action. Ray had been warning Charlie to be careful, but Frankie said something at the right time, and Charlie began to really listen. Charlie looked at Frankie and almost told him what Ray had said about his parents, he so desperately wanted to tell someone. Like an overflowing dam, ready to burst, he sat there with an open mouth ready for the water to come rushing out, but then he paused. Charlie had not dealt with any of this himself and he was still questioning what Ray had told him. He decided to tell Frankie another time. Maybe it was embarrassment, or shock; either way, he closed his mouth. Charlie needed some answers. His life was spiraling out of control; he needed to control his emotions and he needed some answers.

Charlie got up, threw a hundred-dollar bill on the table, and told Frankie that he'd call him later. Charlie stopped by the valet to get his keys and did not wait for them to bring it up. He called Doris to cancel the rest of the afternoon and called Ray from the car. If there was anyone who could locate someone or find out about someone, it would be Ray. That son of a bitch knew everyone.

Ray could do a background check, but he needed some information to start with. Charlie had no pictures, no birth date, no last name, and no place of residence. Ray could do nothing with what he had. It would be an impossible task even for Ray. It was impossible to locate someone if you don't know who you are looking for.

Charlie was fucking lost. He had no idea what to do next. He could pursue Serina, which at this point seemed fruitless no matter how much effort he was willing to give, or he could just move on. He could put it all behind him, write it all off, and re-focus himself on his company and life. Charlie was good at moving on. He does it with business and he could do it with Serina.

After a drive around the lake, he decided to go home. This hurt more than any blown business deal; Charlie was numb inside and out, left without any plausible option. This was Charlie's wake-up call. He made a promise to himself that his head would be straight, from this point forward, no more distractions. This was the best way to get over Serina. The little voice told him to move on, remember the good times, and let those memories fuel the passion to start fresh. The little voice also kept reminding Charlie of those sultry eyes and that velvet sun-kissed skin. Charlie told the voices to shut the fuck up. He needed to get back to what he was; to his true self.

At home, Charlie walked up the stairs, still looking around just waiting for her to reappear. He changed his clothes, picked up the *Wall Street Journal* sitting on his dresser, and went outside on the patio. There was a chill in the air, but he was comfortable wearing a t-shirt and basketball shorts. With the paper in one hand and a Bailey's Irish Cream in the other, he stared off into the distance. As the sun was going down, he couldn't help but glance at this watch. He must have checked the time twice a minute until the sun set, but she never came back. Watching the reflection of the sun disappearing over the blue transparent water, Charlie took a long, purposeful breath and set the paper down. He got up out of the chair and tried to think if Serina had mentioned anything. Talking to himself, even yelling at times, did not seem to wash his memory clean. Nothing came to mind except the memories of an outstanding weekend. Astounded by the events, Charlie went to bed with the hopes that Serina would wake up next to him. She did not. The vow not to think about Serina was going to be harder than he thought, but his options were limited.

A Month Later

"Good morning Mr. Rocklin. Glad to have you back." Doris said.

It took Charlie a good month to get back to his old self that was on the cover of <u>Forbes</u> magazine. The Charlie that was strong, confident, and passionate about the business that made him an extremely wealthy man. Business was first and foremost again. Nothing was standing in his way, and nothing pre-occupying his mind. He had not spoken of Serina in a month. No one spoke of her, and that was the way he wanted it. Charlie was off the grid for an entire month; meetings were pushed, new clients on a waiting list and no returned work calls. A self-imposed rehabilitation to free his mind and to hit refresh.

"Today is busy, but you already knew that. You have the presentation at the Elks Lodge in Chicago on the funding for the next fiscal year. There will be members from the other regional Elks representing the rest of the country. They also want you to give the opening ceremonial speech at their 150-year celebration in San Antonio in early July. Should I bill them at the $500 or $1,000 hourly rate?" Doris asked.

"Do it at $1,000, for the reason that I have to travel to them for the meeting," Charlie responded with a determined tone. All the bullshit was gone, time to make some fucking money!

"Then you are flying to Minnesota to meet and talk to a new venture group that Hobbs and Conner have started. Remember they talked to you about funding last year, but you declined. You had promised to meet with them again to take a look at their position and possible reconsideration of their proposal. I'll put a copy of their presentation deck, current financials and year to date financials, going back a year from today, on your OneDrive. I think it would be best if you stayed in Minnesota for the night, because you are flying to Italy in the morning to meet with the Bonfiglio family. They will have a car at the airport waiting to take you to the meeting and then back to the hotel. They will also be transporting you to the airport in the morning. In addition to Hobbs in Minnesota, I have you meeting with Robert Winkle of Winkle Productions. You are having dinner with him to go over the documentary he would like to do. You will also be meeting with David MacLennan from Cargill. David would like your help in how they provide data analytics, market expertise and financial solutions for their partners. I have put their FY20 annual report on your OneDrive. You'll need to collect a retainer of five hundred thousand if he decides to sign the contract. I'll call him to confirm, and have him wire the funds in the morning. Do you need to break before I go into detail about your Italy trip?"

"No, I'm ready, please continue."

"When you arrive in Rome, Anthony, the eldest son, will pick you up. I haven't booked a room for you, as the family has extended an invitation to stay at their house for the nights you are in town. I have placed their financial statement, year over year, side by side of the investments for the past five years, for your review on your OneDrive. You have tripled their investment returns, each year, year over year, for the past five years. They are also aware of the fee that is due. They are unable to wire the funds so they will be giving you a check for $28 million. I have also put the financial fee statement for your review in the same file. Please review it before giving a copy. The check will come from Resolve Enterprises, and not the family. Then you are back here by Friday afternoon. I have opened up Friday so that you can catch up." Doris spoke very quickly, and Charlie was off to the lodge.

Benevolent and Protective Order of Elks

The Elks was a client that started with Charlie being a guest speaker which turned into one of his longest and most sustainable sources of income. From the outside it was just a large building with a pool. Inside it resembled an empty warehouse with a cutout

for the kitchen. Often rented for various events and
conventions, the Elks Lodge is well known. When one
thinks of the Elks Lodge, one may think of the charitable
contributions they make in their respective communities,
or youth programs they sponsor, or college scholarships
they offer or a place to rent for a special occasion.
Income or large sums of money are not synonymous
with the Benevolent and Protective Order of Elks. But
with over 2 million members, 2000 regional offices, and a
150-year history, the Elks are probably one of the most
underrated liquid money machines in this country.
Quite often they own outdated buildings with older
pools and not much personality, and that is precisely the
impression the Elks want you to have. What most
people do not know is that it is a member only club, a
fraternal organization that only accepts new members by
referral from an existing member in good standing.

They are a well-established, deep-rooted, wealthy, and organized institution that is operated, run and controlled through a member's board. Charlie had to become a Freemason before they would entrust him with their finances. He has been a Master Mason for over 20 years.

Financially, the Elks organization has one of the most profitable business structures on the planet, with an enormous cash reserve. The Elks have vast portfolios of stocks, bonds, property holdings and other investments. Additionally, each regional chapter may acquire property and other investments, as long as it is in the best interest of the lodge and its members. Each investment, every building improvement, every property acquisition, must be approved by the board and in turn, must be given the final approval by the investment advisor, Charlie Rocklin. Charlie was the first financial advisor ever hired by the Elks. Each building is insured for 3 million dollars with over 2000

buildings throughout the United States. Each board

member or partner must have a buy-sell policy with a

face amount of $4 million, there are 25 board members.

For an organization that spends over 80 million dollars a

year for various programs and scholarships, their income

is greater than 99.9% of the American public. With last

year's income greater than $800 million, that is just 10%

of their net profits. Much of their income is derived from

member dues, donations, property valuation, stocks,

futures and short-term and long-term investments.

Charlie has been responsible for doubling their annual

income over the past 10 years. There is more scrutiny on

the properties that are acquired. The investments are

made with long term growth potential rather than short-

term gain.

Every year, Charlie does a portfolio review with

the board. Within that review, Charlie has a comparative market analysis done on every piece of land and buildings that are on that land. He looks at the year over year returns on the investments and interest that they are making for that investment. Preparation for the annual review takes two months and the review with the board takes another two weeks to complete. Handling and caring for this 1 customer takes roughly 20% of Charlie's time on an annual basis. In addition to the Elks organization as a whole, Charlie also provides his financial services to over 80% of the members of the board. And because of the amount of time, he invests in the Elks, Charlie collects somewhere north of 60 million dollars a year.

Italy

Every year, Charlie flies to Italy to meet with the

heads of the Bonfiglio family, one of the strongest mafia families in the world, and not only in terms of brute strength. Primarily based in Northern Italy, they have branch offices all over the world. Their businesses include restaurants, grocery stores, bars, liquor depots, mail stops, check cashing, pawn shops, furniture stores, ISP providers, and of course, waste management. The diversity was structured to enable a cash flow that was not easily traced. The bookkeeping is a tremendous job and is handled by two very discreet individuals. The record accounts are very detailed and are copied with every transaction. The paper trail is coded and washed in a way that is completely untraceable.

Charlie was hired five years ago after the article in the <u>Wall Street Journal</u>. The <u>Journal</u> called Charlie "the man of the century" with regard to financial independence and security. You pay for what you get,

and if you can afford the services of Charlie Rocklin,
then chances are you are going to find financial
independence along the road, no matter what that road
looked like. The Bonfiglio's knew they needed the kind
of services Charlie had to offer, but their kind of business
was not business Charlie was keen on helping. There is
a price for everything, and the less Charlie knew about
the family business, the better. Little did Charlie know,
but the Bonfiglio family had been following Charlie very
closely for the past 30-years. They knew where he went
to school, who he talked to, who he was friends with,
and most importantly, they knew Charlie's parents.

The Bonfiglio name has been around for 200
years. With a reputation in organized crime, it was often
difficult to build a financial portfolio for the next
generation. The largest effort was trying to find
legitimate businesses, while still engaging in the

"business" that was started all those years ago with Vincent Bonfiglio. Year after year, business after business and having to deal with untimely deaths in the family, pieces of the puzzle began to fall. This left the family open to extortion, investigations, arrests, and other forms of threat. Even though they have existed for the last 200 years, they called upon the services of Charlie to creatively create, yet simplify businesses, and to secure a future that was not only financially worthy, but relatively safe compared to what Vince started back in the early 1800's. Were they going all in on the legitimate side of the law, and turn their entire operation over to a competitor? Not fucking likely.

For two centuries, they have found a way to make a lot of money and most of that continues to this day. But it was Charlie who made the Bonfiglio's more business-oriented with legal endeavors rather than take their chances with illegal operations. Charlie's involvement with the Bonfiglio's has never been made public. Before Charlie officially met with the family five years ago, a waiver was signed to indemnify him of any wrongdoing. Charlie "knew" nothing of the family, and was just providing financial planning and investments services, just as he does for all of his other clients. The only difference between this relationship and the ones he had with his other clients, is that if shit went sideways, Charlie could wake up next to the head of a horse or not even wake up at all. Charlie knew the risks involved, but the annual financial gain of $200 million dollars was worth the calculated risk. Unlike a cash retainer that he collects from his other clients, Charlie is paid in various forms. He may get a random check in the mail, a deed to a piece of property, the title to an island, a new car, or other forms of equity. Charlie knew how to build a wealth portfolio for his clients, but he also knew how to

build a varied portfolio for himself.

Charlie implemented a plan that he considers one

of his best. The challenge was the limited resources he

had available to help put the plan in place. Due to the

sensitive nature of the plan and the client, Charlie had to

do much of the implementation himself. Diversification

was the key, as well as maintaining an accurate

transaction record with checks and balances. A

consistent balance sheet with payables, receivables,

assets and liabilities and a means of collection, if

necessary. Angelo was the designated accountant who

lived in Italy, and he was a member of the family. He

was the only one, aside from Charlie, who knew the

books, money and businesses that were created or

purchased. Having only one person assigned, was a

way to ensure there was no confusion who was

accountable if any mistakes were made. And having Angelo as that one person, it was easy to take care of business, if that time should ever come. Charlie meets with Angelo and the Bonfiglio's once a year, to go over each business entity, the financials for each one, address or entertain any other business ventures that are brought up, legal ones, and then reports back on projections for the upcoming year. They fly him to their hometown in Italy and invite him to stay in their house, a 25-room mansion on 125 acres in a remote part of Northern Italy. Anthony, the patriarch, and decision-maker, would never invite a guest without showing the hospitality by extending an invitation to stay at his house. Charlie has never refused that offer. For five years now, Charlie has become a regular fixture in the Bonfiglio family. Gaining trust from these guys is something that you cannot purchase.

One month before his annual trip, Charlie is

hand-delivered all the necessary information to do his

review and come up with recommendations. Two

gentlemen, representatives of the family, fly into Tahoe

to hand Charlie a large envelope of material, and then fly

out. They are not on the ground for longer than 30

minutes, before turning around to go home back to Italy.

In this envelope are all the businesses, financial

transactions from those businesses, deposits, and

withdrawals from each of their 18 bank accounts, from

all over the world. It takes Charlie two full weeks to

perform his review, come up with questions, and make

his recommendations. On this one account, no one else

touches or even knows about the information. He

handles everything himself. Doris knows the Bonfiglio

family is a client but does not have any other

information.

Once in Italy, his trip usually lasts seven days. The first and last days are social days. Business is never discussed on the first day. Charlie arrives and is escorted to the mansion by several armed employees. There is a big dinner and party to welcome their guest, filled with great food, lots of wine and plenty of cigars. Day two is strictly business, with the meeting starting promptly at 9:00 in the morning. The only ones present at the meeting are Anthony, his two sons, and the consigliere. Charlie first hears from Anthony on how he felt about the previous year. He hears all the concerns and takes down any questions Anthony had. He also entertains any other business ideas, ventures or changes Anthony wants to make. With meals, this usually consumes the majority of day two. Day three is all Charlie. And while Charlie can make suggestions or changes to the plans, Anthony always has the final word, no questions asked.

Charlie puts more effort into this particular presentation than any other due to the risks involved. The proposal is usually a few hundred pages detailing everything from historical data from the past year, compared to the previous two years, followed by recommendations for the coming year. The investment section is 50 pages alone and outlines every single deposit and payment from all the different accounts. He also provides financial statements for the financial institutions that are handling the money in order to give the assurance of stability and reports any changes with board and executive leaders within those banks. This process consumes the entire third and fourth days.

Finally, on day five, Charlie gives an overview of his recommendations, and they discuss any changes or concerns they have. No matter how much money is passing through each bank or how many line items are on the account statements, Anthony likes to review each one, line by line. He accounts for every penny that is deposited or withdrawn, and is aware of every single transaction the family makes. Nothing, absolutely nothing gets done without Anthony's blessing. Day five ends with all the presentations and recommendations turned over to the consigliere for one final review. All documents that were delivered to Charlie the month prior, as well as all of Charlie's material are handed over. Nothing leaves the house. On Charlie's last day in Italy, the morning is for signing, followed by a goodbye lunch and an escort back to the airstrip from which Charlie came.

For the week, Charlie is given a check for $10 million dollars, and over the next year, he will be paid in various forms. The $10 million is for his time, effort and being that trusted advisor. The additional payments are

for his continued confidence, knowing Charlie would

never jeopardize their relationship. And if he ever did,

they would know, and he would then have something

other than Serina to worry about.

Chapter Ten

Driving home in his Aston Martin Vantage Volante, Charlie enjoys the drive. It is getting late and he was coming home from dinner with Frankie. It was 11:30 on Friday night. As Charlie pulls into his driveway to access the gate, he noticed it was open already. Given the secure codes required for access to the gates, and that he never got a notification, them being opened was of concern to Charlie. As he passes through the gate, he stops just inside and watches it close behind him. Pulling slowly up the driveway, he puts the brights on to get a better view. Nothing seems to be out of the ordinary as he winds through the driveway and approaches the main house. Just as he turned the corner to open the garage door, he saw a red convertible Jaguar parked in front of it. The license plate of the car read "MISSME." Charlie knew who the visitor was. Time has come and gone, and he had not heard from Serina in six months. He has almost doubled his earnings since this time last year and has re-dedicated himself to his business. He had put Serina out of his mind. Charlie was a new man. He was temporarily veered off track, but has regained his former glory, and now this. A part of him wanted it to be her, and the other part was hoping it was not.

He parked his car behind the mysterious convertible, turned off his engine, and sat with his mind racing. Over the past six months, he has done everything possible to forget Serina. He has re-focused his life and made a promise to himself and his staff that there will be no other distractions. That promise was easy to keep considering his focus and attention to what is important in his life. He had to get his life back in control. Even though he still loved Serina, he had to forget her. But what about now? Charlie knew he was in trouble. He knew his heart was not ready to face her. He knew the feelings were still there. He did not want to confront Serina; not now, not ever. Charlie did not want to return to that place.

Charlie took the keys from his hand and started the car. As he drove down the driveway, he could not help but wonder what she was doing back in his life, if it was in fact Serina. He did not want to find out. He called Frankie.

"Frankie, you are not going to believe who is at my house."

"A playmate? Do you want me to come over and help you out? Maybe a little tag?" Frankie said sarcastically.

"No, it's Serina."

"You're fucking kidding me! Did you talk to her?"

"As I pulled into the house, there was a car parked outside with the license plate that read 'MISSME'. Who else could that be?" Charlie said.

"So, you didn't see who it was? How are you so sure it's her?"

"Frankie, I just know. I have this gut feeling that it's her. I can't deal with this right now. I'm not ready," Charlie admitted.

"Come on down, I'll wait for you."

As Charlie drove to meet Frankie at the restaurant, his mind was a fucking mess. Thoughts were going all over. As he pulled up to Rotchedo's, Frankie was waiting outside with two drinks and two Cuban cigars.

"You have got to be fucking kidding me Charlie. What in the world is she doing back here?"

"If I only knew. God damn her," Charlie said.

Frankie knew by his friend's demeanor that Serina was not forgotten. Out of sight, but surely not forgotten. She might have been placed in the back somewhere, on a shelf inside a box, but from this reaction, she was alive as ever. Serina was a hard habit to break. Charlie still loved her, and it showed in his trembling hands.

"What am I going to do? What are my options at this point?"

"Listen, Serina was once a part of your life. When she left, you had no idea why. Maybe she was feeling too close to you. Maybe it was all moving too fast. A little time is all she needed. You have no idea what happened because you are here. You can stay here rather than go inside to find out why she left, if in fact it is her. You still feel for her; I can see that deep down you want to see her, you want to be with her. If nothing else, you need closure. Shit, listen to me man, I'm sounding like a chick. I can give you my advice all night, but this is something that I can't help you with Charlie. All I want for you is to be happy. As much as I am angry at Serina and I don't want to see you get hurt, I really think you need to face her, if it is really her at the house. I am not a big fan of someone who plays with your heart, but you need to get some closure, you need to seal that box for good. If you think you can see her and keep an open mind, then what's the harm in just seeing her and finding out why she left? I'm not telling you to pick up where you left off, and hell, I should be telling you to just stay here and hope she goes away for good, but I know how hurt you are man. I know with what you went through, you will approach it in a

different manner. I don't know her and I'm not sure I

want to, because I really don't trust her, but I trust you. I

want you to be happy, and I do know that she made you

happy, but you'd better start thinking with the right

head this time. Know what your plan is, before you do

anything. Then again, that might not even be her, we

could be talking about something that will never

happen. Let's go find out, together. Find out what

happened six months ago. I will be with you man, if you

want, if that is what you need." Frankie rested.

"I hear you. But I'm not ready to face her."

"Honestly, I hope it's not her. But if it is, you

owe it to yourself to just have some answers. It is your

fucking house. At the very least, go home and kick her

ass out, if it really is Serina and if that's really what you

want. Just don't make the same mistake twice. And if it

is her, you need to find out who the fuck she really is.

Have her fill out an employment application or

something, so you can get some information about her."

Frankie was a good friend, who always had an

objective outlook on things. Charlie was unable to see

the other side, but Frankie did. Frankie gave advice

from someone on the outside looking in, rather than

having a tainted viewpoint. This was a big decision that

he had to make. Just going home was a big decision. He

had opened himself up before and got burned; was he

willing to do it again, with the same person? The answer

was in the affirmative as Charlie started the Aston and

drove home. Charlie told Frankie he wanted to go alone,

against what Frankie suggested, but he would call, if

needed.

Pulling up to the driveway, Charlie went through

a hundred scenarios as to what happened six months

ago and now, what to say to her. It was time to face those possibilities and face Serina. He had so many questions and needed closure to move on. Turning the car off, Charlie got out and began his walk up the front door. Just as he was about ten feet away, the door opened and there stood Serina in a short, see-through red sheer dress. She wasn't wearing anything else.

Charlie's heart came out of his shirt. He blinked fast, as if he could not believe she was standing there. Charlie stopped in his tracks and just looked at the person in front of his eyes. Just like the first time he laid eyes on her, he was frozen. Serina was just as beautiful as when she disappeared. She started to walk toward Charlie, and he took a step backward. Was he ready for this all over again? Doubts filled his mind and he turned around and headed toward the car. Feeling for his keys in his pocket, he opened the door, but Serina was right behind him. Just as he was going to sit down, she put her hand on his back and took hold of his waist. Charlie stopped, smelling her scent once again. As the memories rushed into his brain, he put his head on the door of the car. Serina held him tight and did not let go. She whispered in his ear, "I'm sorry." That was it for Charlie; once he heard her voice, he was taken back. He turned around, looked into her seemingly endless eyes, and kissed her lips. Tears started to roll down Serina's face, and Charlie wiped them with his thumb. Fighting back the flood of emotions, Charlie was angry, anxious, nervous, scared, and excited, all at once.

"I missed you so much," Charlie said.

"I missed you too Charlie."

As they went inside, he had to ask. Even though he had other things on his mind, Charlie had to have some answers.

"Serina, what happened?"

"I had to clear up some issues in my life. I was so messed up then. I was confused. You were the last person I wanted to hurt, but I had to go. I had to see my dad; he is not doing well," Serina said as she looked into his eyes.

"Why did you just leave? You could have told me or even asked me for help; I would have done anything for you, you know that. When you left, I was a disaster. You took a part of me that I will never get back."

"Charlie, I know, I'm so sorry, but I needed to work this out on my own. But now I'm back. Now I'm with you again," She said.

"I know you are back, but how long will that last? I cannot give to this what I did before, and get nothing in return. I cannot afford to open myself up again, and have you leave again. How can I trust you that you will not walk out like before? Honestly, I don't think I can do this again, I'm sorry." Charlie said.

"You can trust me. I'm here to stay, or at least until you want me to leave. Unless you want me to leave right now." Serina said as she glanced at her suitcase with puppy-dog eyes.

"I'm sorry, I just can't," Charlie said as he sat in his car.

Charlie put the key into the ignition and started the car, then he drove away, watching Serina in his rearview mirror. Charlie took a long drive around the lake. No music, just the wind blowing through his hair. The drive around the lake usually takes an hour, with no traffic. It took Charlie two hours before he pulled back into his driveway. Serina was there, sitting on the front porch, shivering from the cold.

"What are you doing here? You should leave and get warm."

"No, I'm not leaving you again. I made a mistake, and I cannot walk away from you. I should have told you, I know that, but I'm not leaving Charlie," Serina said as she wiped away her tears.

"Come inside. Let's sit in front of the fire."

Charlie and Serina sat across from each other on the circular couch that was surrounding the fireplace.

"OK, I don't want you to leave. I want you in my life, but if you are going to stay, you will need to do something for me," Charlie said as he got up and headed to the kitchen.

"I will do anything for you, just ask me."

Charlie sat next to Serina with a paper in one hand and a pen in the other.

"You want to stay? Then I will need you to write

down everything I don't know about you, right now. I want to know your last name, I want to know the names of your parents, where you grew up, and what your phone number is."

Serina knew the only way she was going to be able to keep this man, was to do exactly that he asked. She took the pen and paper and began writing down all her information.

Charlie hugged Serina with both arms and kissed her once more. With a smile, he invited her out on the deck to the hot tub. Charlie was willing to let Serina back into his life, glancing down at the sheet of paper that had a lot of writing on it. The touch of her body, the taste of her skin, Charlie would never be the same.

Awakened by the phone, Charlie picked up the line.

"Is that you, Charlie Rocklin?" said the voice on

the other end.

"Ray, do you have any idea what time it is?" Charlie asked.

"Sure, I do, but this is the only way I ever get to talk to you. I have not heard from you in months; you are one busy man. What is new with your life? Any new news to share with an old friend?" Ray asked as if he knew something.

"I'm kind of busy right now, can I call you later?" Charlie posed the question.

"A girl? That is not like you Charlie. But I am so happy to hear that, my man. Fucking the Serina right out of you. I love it!" Ray said in an enthusiastic voice. There was silence on the other end.

"Wait a fucking minute. Is it Serina? Please tell me it is not her." Ray asked with concern.

A chill overcame Charlie's body. He could hear

the shaking in Ray's voice. Ray always seemed to have the edge on everything, and this was no exception. He always called at the opportune moment; call it intuition. Charlie heard concern and apprehension in Ray's voice. Ray knew something or had a feeling about something, and Charlie needed to find out what.

"Yes Ray, it is, but I need something from you, pretty important. I can't talk right now, but I will be in touch soon. I promise." Charlie hung up the phone.

Charlie was conflicted. His heart was screaming for Serina, but his mind was trying to tell him otherwise. Charlie had heard everything Ray said, but he was never really listening, until now. Fear was beginning to take over. He was even fearing for his life. Investing this much time into one person, and not truly knowing the person, was starting to sink in. Charlie was definitely conflicted. As he laid his head down on the pillow,

Serina turned over and kissed him. Reluctantly, he

accepted her invitation and got on top of her; Charlie

would be going into the office late tomorrow morning.

Chapter Eleven

Charlie woke up early the next morning and got out of bed. Serina was still sleeping, as he made his way downstairs to call Ray.

"Good morning and sorry about last night."

"Don't apologize to me, I just hope you know what you are doing."

"That I don't. But I do need something, a favor. When Serina came back, I had her write down her information. If I send this to you, can you do a little checking for me. Find out who she is, where she came from?" Charlie asked.

"Of course, that is what I am good at Charlie. When can you send it over?"

"Taking a picture now and sending it. Thank

you and just call me when you have something!" Charlie hung up the phone and felt a calmness.

Feeling better about the situation knowing that Ray was on the case, Charlie wasted no time about the new beginning with Serina, he began to plan a week-long getaway. With the assistance of Doris, they planned a trip that most can only dream of. Leaving on a Sunday morning, they would fly to Rio de Janeiro, Brazil, and stay in one of Charlie's cottages in Copacabana overlooking the Atlantic Ocean. After a day on the beach and shopping, they would climb aboard the yacht and sail for the night. In the morning, a helicopter will pick them up and take them to the airport, where the plane will be waiting to take them to Costa Rica. Charlie has a house in Limón that is camouflaged with Allspice trees, filling the air with the amazing scent. Not often visited due to time constraints, Charlie will be traveling there more often, now that he has a reason to.

After the Costa Rica journey, Charlie left the last leg of the trip up to Serina. Wherever she wanted to travel, anywhere in the world, Charlie would take her there. Charlie called Ray for an update after his planning with Doris, but he didn't have any news to report.

This was an exciting time for Charlie. His business could not be better, and his personal life is exactly what he has been wishing for. He has seemed to forget how Serina left months ago without saying a word. He was willing to overlook that little detail and make the best of what time he has with her, determined as he was, to do anything to keep her. He always had the goal to succeed in business; now he could focus on the other part of this life that makes him happy. Even if he stopped working today, Charlie would never have to worry about money, no matter how he spent it. He has made the Forbes richest people in the world the last three years, with an estimated net worth of 25 billion dollars. An amazing feat considering Rocklin and Roll Investments and Consulting is not even 10 years old. He appears in the Wall Street Journal every week with strategic investment tips and market recommendations. He is Time's financial consultant and Newsweek's investment manager. Charlie could afford to take some time off.

"Charlie, I know I promised not to interfere with your personal life, but I have to say that I'm concerned," Doris said.

"Now why would you be concerned about me?"

"I don't know Serina that well, and I don't think you do, either. I think you need to get to know her a little better before you start re-organizing your life. You did this one other time, and look how that turned out,"

Doris said in a concerned voice.

"I have talked about this with Serina. I feel that

she is the one. I know she feels the same. I did promise

you that I would get no other distractions, and I have

called Ray, and he is looking into her background. That

alone helps me sleep at night. Today is not like last time,

I am making sure of that," Charlie explained.

"It has been six weeks. Do you feel that you

know her better now than you did six months ago?

Have you met her parents, brothers, or sisters? What is

her last name? Where is she from? What does she do?

Does she even have a job? What do you really know

about her?" Doris asked.

"Wait a second. This does not sound like a Doris

line of questioning. It sounds like you've been talking to

Ray," Charlie stated.

"Yes, Ray has been calling. He is deeply concerned for you, as am I."

"I completely understand your concerns and Ray's, for that matter. I have talked to Ray and he is looking into a few things. I am just waiting for him to call back with any news. Can you please get Ray on the phone?"

Charlie stood up and went towards the window overlooking the lake, waiting for Doris' announcement.

"I have Ray on line 1," Doris said through the speaker.

"Ray, you know I'm impatient when it comes to certain things, please tell me you have something to report?" Charlie asked.

"Well, hello to you, my friend. No hello, thank you, or any other pleasantries, just getting down to business I see," Ray responded.

"Yes, sorry, hello and how are you doing?"

Charlie said.

"Better, thank you. And yes, I have some information on Serina. I was able to find a little bit of information before you gave me all her details, and now, I'm able to tell you what I know and what I have found out," Ray explained.

"Excellent! I am all ears. Speak to me," Charlie said with a little excitement.

"Charlie, you are one of the most influential people in the world. You are a public figure in the financial arena and have a shit load of money. I read the papers; I get the magazines. I know what they say about you and who you are. Has it ever occurred to you that this woman is after just one thing? She appears, then disappears, and then like fucking magic, she is back." Ray said.

"I know how it might appear, that is why I am asking for your help. And no, Serina is not after my money, she is harmless. So, what did you find?" Charlie asked.

"Charlie, you are wrong. First of all, she is not harmless, at least I don't think she is. Second, I did not mention this before because I was having a hard time getting the information. Remember the night I came to town, and we went to Frankie's place? After I left, I pulled up the license plate on the car that Serina was driving. It is registered to her mother."

Charlie interrupted, "Her mother, Ray, so what, she has a mother, I think I already knew that."

"Listen you smartass, you are not listening to me. It is registered to her mother, but her mother died over a year ago."

"So what? Her mother died a year ago, what

does that have to do with anything?"

"This is where the information that you sent me helped me piece the puzzle together. Do you know what her mother's name is?"

After a slight pause, Charlie responded, "No."

"Her mother's name was Mary Rothwell. Serina's last name is Rothwell, Charlie. Don't you find it a little strange that a year ago, I had a detective at my door, re-investigating an unsolved mystery about the death of Peter Rothwell? And then Serina appears into your life right after her mother dies? Is she so harmless now?" Ray said in a voice Charlie had never heard before.

"So, her mother dies and I meet her, what is wrong with that?" Charlie reluctantly asked.

Charlie sat down in his office chair, letting the reality of the situation sink in. He wanted to argue the facts, but he was growing concerned with every word

Ray was speaking. A part of him wanted to just hang up

the phone and pretend he never heard the news from

Ray. Another part of him was angry, upset and

confused as to why Serina suddenly appeared in his life.

"Are you really going to sit there and pretend

this is just a coincidence? That this woman just happens

to 'find' you? Just runs into you out of nowhere? Come

on Charlie, you cannot be serious right now, brother."

"So, I guess that makes Serina's father, Peter

Rothwell?" Charlie said as he could barely get the

words out.

Charlie was completely numb. His hands began

to tremble. He swallowed hard several times, just to

force his own saliva down his throat. Chills ran up his

body from his head to his feet.

"Why the fuck do you think she found me? Do

you really think she's after me? She obviously knew

who my parents were, but why would someone want to

find *me*, for something I had nothing to do with?"

"Charlie, I think you should come to Florida. It

will give you some time away and to think about this. I

am still digging and should have a few more answers or

information when you get here."

Charlie had to go to Florida. For more than a

year, Ray had been trying to tell him something, and this

was it. Ray only had pieces and never the whole picture,

until now. Charlie needed more answers.

"I will see you in the morning, I will fly to Florida

to see you, meet me at hanger 15 at 10:00 a.m." Charlie

hung up the phone.

Charlie sat there behind his desk for over an

hour, replaying the conversation in his head. He was

feeling used, saddened and mostly in disbelief. Charlie

did not want to believe what Ray had told him, but he knew it was the truth, or at least part of the truth. As Charlie sat behind his desk, he wanted to believe that Serina was different and that it was that one out of a million chance that she had no ulterior motives and that she truly loved him. There was only one way to find out and that was to confront Serina with the news and ask her side of the story. She did lie to him about her father and that fueled the doubts in Charlie's mind. He knows what he should do, but Charlie wanted this to be real, to be authentic and he believed, deep down, that no matter what Serina was really doing there, that he could change that. He packed up his belongings and headed home

Charlie opened the front door. Serina was standing in the entryway with one of his shirts on. It was dark, except for the lights from the steps on the stairs illuminating Serina's outline.

"How was your day honey?" Serina asked as she tilted her head to one side.

With a forced smile, Charlie said.

"It was an interesting day. Not as good as coming home to you and seeing you standing there!" Charlie ran his hands threw his hair and approached Serina.

Taking her by the hand, he led her to the couch in the living room.

"I have to ask you something and I would like you to be honest with me," Charlie said as he was looking Serina in the eyes.

"Yes, I will try. What is on your mind," she responded.

"Where are your parents right now?"

"My parents? Why is that bothering you?"

"You didn't answer the question."

"Well, my mother passed away last year."

Silence filled the air.

"And, your father?"

"Do you know what happened to my father?" Serina asked back.

"What is your father's name? And you said the reason why you left was to be with your father, but I find that hard to believe."

"My mother was Mary and my father was Peter."

"Rothwell?" Charlie asked.

"Yes, Mary and Peter Rothwell. My father is not alive." Serina said as she wiped away her tears.

"Charlie, I did not want to lie to you, but when I went home last month, it was not to visit my father. I had to take care of a few things from my mother's estate. And my father, what did you hear about my father?" Serina probed.

"I know of a Peter Rothwell that disappeared sometime ago in Las Vegas, but that is all I really know, or what I had been told." Charlie said.

Serina was having trouble sitting still and had to get up and walk. Charlie watched her walk around the couch, still wiping the tears from her face. He sat on the couch deciding how far to go with the questions. How much more information did he want to get out of Serina tonight?

"Are you alright? Do you want to stop talking about this right now?" Charlie asked.

"I'm sorry for not telling you the truth," Serina said as she made her way back to the couch.

"If you still have questions, I will try and answer them. I want you to know who I am, I want to you know everything about me, so if you have anything else you want to ask me, then feel free."

"I think that is enough for one night," Charlie said, wiping the remaining tear from Serina's cheek.

"Let's just go upstairs and call it a night. We can continue this another time," Charlie said.

The Next Morning

As the clock struck 7:30 a.m., there was a knock at the door.

"Charlie, are you awake? I need to speak to you," Brian said.

Charlie put on his robe and went to open the door.

"What is it?"

"Ray has called twice, wondering where you are. Doris has also called to see when you were coming in. And your Aston Martin has been delivered." Brian updated Charlie on the day's events.

Charlie had always wanted an Aston Martin

Lagonda, the four-door saloon produced in the late seventies and eighties. Not your typical Aston Martin and Charlie will be spending more money on repairs than the price he paid for the car, but it was just one of those cars that spoke to Charlie.

Charlie went to the phone and called Doris.

"Good morning. How is everything?" Charlie asked.

"Nice to hear from you. Will you be coming in this morning?"

"I will be there within the hour, not to worry."

"Ray has called for you, saying you were going to fly to Florida. Did you tell me about this trip?"

"No, when I talked to Ray yesterday, I told him I would be down there in the morning, but I can't make it. Can you please call him and let him know that I will set up another time. Right now, is just not good for me. See you soon. I will be on the cell if you need me."

Charlie went back to the bedroom to let Serina know he was going to take a shower. The day after tomorrow, Charlie was taking Serina on their week-long trip, and he could hardly wait. It will also be a good time to pick up the conversation from the night before. After a steam shower, Charlie dressed for the day in casual attire, knowing that Doris would be clearing his calendar for the week. Doris had to pull some magic out of her ass to clear Charlie's calendar with a days' notice, but she would succeed. Charlie took the Aston Martin that was waiting right outside his door.

Upon driving into his parking space in the front of the building, Charlie's cell phone rang, it was Ray.

"Charlie, what the fuck is going on? You have your secretary call me to tell me you will not be coming here, and two hours after the fact. What are you" as

Charlie interrupted.

"Ray, I was talking with Serina last night and getting more details. I wanted to get a few more answers from her before I came out." Charlie said.

"Ok, that is fair. Have you asked her about her parents?" Ray asked.

"Yes, she told me her mother passed away a year ago and that her father had passed years ago. We did not get into any details yet, but I plan on doing that in the next few days."

"And she told you who her father was, right?"

"She told me her father was Peter Rothwell."

"Alright, well, let me know what else you find out. I really don't like you being alone with her right now. With everything we know right now, it just seems too coincidental, and I am a little worried about what she might have planned for you."

"Thank you, Ray, I do appreciate that, but you don't need to worry about me. I am taking it with caution and will call you when I know more." And Charlie hung up the phone.

Ray had a feeling that was not good. He could not, for certain, tell Charlie, until he knew a little more information, but he wanted Charlie to know to be careful with Serina. Ray was the detective; he has seen this before. It was not difficult to find out that Peter Rothwell had had a daughter, and it was not difficult to track where she was, but now that she is on the move, Ray's mission was going to get more involved. He had to phone a friend.

The first order of business was to contact his buddy at the Las Vegas Sheriff's office to get background info on the Rothwell's, the disappearance and death of Peter, the circumstances around the recent death of Mary

Rothwell, and their children, most notably, the daughter, Serina. If you know who to call and what questions to ask, getting information on someone was a relatively easy task, especially for someone like Ray.

Ray started in Vegas and talked to the same person who informed him about Serina and the registered owner of the car. Ray knew it was a little suspicious that he was visited by a detective just months before Serina entered Charlie's life. After her mysterious disappearance, Ray made a few calls and found out her true identity. Not that it was a huge discovery or even difficult to get, but he needed at least two pieces of information; the license plate and the information that Charlie had sent, was all he needed. Charlie was a hard businessman; and anyone who tried to tell him how to run his business would be quickly pushed aside, and that was what he was doing with Ray. Charlie believed what Ray was saying, but now he needed to do things his way and find out why. But unlike Charlie's clients, Ray was not going anywhere. Ray had made a career of finding people and not strictly following orders. He was not about to buckle to Charlie. He loved the challenge, and he was determined to protect Charlie, even if Charlie did not want to be protected.

After a short day at the office, Charlie met Serina for lunch at a restaurant within walking distance. It was a local sandwich shop called Between the Buns. A little hole in the wall that was popular with the locals and during the lunch hour, it was standing room only. Charlie got there early and sat at a table next to the window, so he could see when Serina arrived. Serina pulled up in her convertible, and Charlie watched passionately, as she parked the car. Just the sight of her made his heart accelerate, even if it was just a lunch date.

This was hard for Charlie. His heart was telling him one

thing and his mind another. Most people in this

situation would run, and never look back. But not

Charlie, he was determined to find out the truth. Charlie

believes, in his heart, that he has found his one true love

in Serina and no matter what she has done or who tried

to talk him out of it, he needed to do it his way. Charlie

was fully prepared to do whatever it took to make sure

Serina was there to stay. He would give up everything

that he had worked so hard for, give it up without a

second thought, but he was still conflicted.

Preparing for their getaway, Charlie was getting

that nervous feeling again. Although it is an odd feeling

to have for such a grounded man, he likes it. It makes

him feel as if he was in grade school watching a girl from

the back of the room. For someone who has been around

the block or even who owns the block, the sensation of

love was new to him. As they packed their bags, Charlie could not help but stare at Serina. He watched her every move. He watched as she put her clothes into the suitcase; he watched her hands; her head as she turned to look in the drawers, and her body. Infatuation was the best word to describe it.

Once everything was all packed and the bags were loaded into the car, the driver took them to the airport; where his plane was waiting. Dinner was onboard with a bottle of Louis Roederer Brut Champagne chilling next to two Tiffany flutes: a perfect start to what would be a perfect vacation. Only Doris knew where they were going, and that was the only person who was going to know. Charlie was available on cell phone for emergency purposes only.

Chapter Twelve

Ray called Las Vegas Sheriff Deputy, Bill Peterson. Bill and Ray have known one another for over 30 years. They were both in the academy together and served as partners in the FBI. Even when Ray decided to go into private practice and leave the FBI, he and Bill would help each other out from time to time. Bill had the ability to perform background checks on individuals with his access to federal-only accessible data sources. This may not be technically official FBI business, but Bill also knew if he needed street information, Ray was able to get it for him. Bill retired from the Bureau and was doing consultant work for the sheriff's department until they asked him to get involved on complex murder investigations. Bill has been with the Vegas Sheriff's office for 15 years and had been able to solve cases that had previously been left open or declared unsolved. Bill has been approached multiple times to run for sheriff, but he was not a political man. He was done with the spotlight, and wanted to keep his life as simple as he could.

Ray wanted to forget everything he *thought* he knew, start at the beginning, and ask why he was questioned when Mary Rothwell passed away. He knew by asking that first, Bill would get into the death of Peter and that is ultimately what Ray needed. Mary passed away a year and a half ago. The case remained open at the Sheriff's office, due to her financial contributions to the department. At the time of Peter Rothwell's death, there were no suspects, until Rocco gave them one. For the next 30 years, Mary questioned everything Rocco said and never once believed that Jansen alone, killed her husband. Mary had a feeling someone else was involved, but could never prove anything. It was her money and persistence that kept the file open.

Once the department got word of Mary's death, they sent a young detective to officially close the case. There was no sense in sending a seasoned detective to ask one question on a case that already had a conviction, so the rookie got the job. Once he satisfied his curiosity with questioning certain individuals, including Ray, the case was closed and filed away. Ray was one of two people questioned due to the information gathered from Mary years prior. In the file that was filled with very little paper and very little evidence, other than the testimony of Rocco and conviction of Jansen, there were two names listed on a piece of paper. Ray was one of them. Mary was always suspicious of Aaron, and even more of Ray, but nothing ever came of it except a name on a white piece of paper. After the murder trial of

Jansen, legally the case was closed. A person had been convicted and sentenced, but Mary still had her doubts and those doubts followed her to her grave.

For the next thirty years, Mary called the Sheriff's department on the anniversary of Peter's disappearance and asked them if they had any other leads or suspects that could be questioned. There were 30 pages, one for every phone call from Mary, representing 30 years. And year after year, the same write-up ended up on the piece of paper and filed away. In simple terms; disappearance, testimony, body found, conviction, and a sentence. Even with the advancement of technology and DNA tests, they were still not able to link Aaron, Sandra, or Ray to what really happened to Peter Rothwell. The case was closed after the guilty verdict, but re-opened at Mary's request, two years later. Mary stated that she had some new evidence about the case, but as time went on, it was easy to tell why the case remained open for all these years. With every call from Mary, there also came a check. With budget cuts and administrative layoffs, these checks were welcomed with open arms, and with that, came the open case.

After Peter's disappearance, Mary was distraught and did not have any family to help console her grieving. She was alone with two little children, and not many friends to help. Having nowhere else to turn, she began a relationship with Stan Stanley, who was presiding as the chief of police at the time of Peter's disappearance investigation. After the initial investigation turned up no leads or suspects, Mary and Stan began to date and eventually got married. Being the wife of the chief had its advantages, but even then, that was unable to clear her doubts about who she thought was behind the death of her Peter. Peter was her husband, her first true love and the father of her children. His disappearance and subsequent death only made Mary's pure hatred for Charlie's parents that much greater. Stan and Mary discussed the investigation and trial often, but no matter what Stan did, it was not enough to satisfy Mary. That was unacceptable to Mary and this caused additional stress on Stan. Soon his health began to deteriorate, but Mary would not let up. They may have been married, but Mary was persistent that the Rocklin's, or someone they associated with had something to do with the case. Stan was not able to do much to ease her mind.

After Stan died of a heart attack, it was his influence that keep the case alive along with Mary's constant calls and contributions. Stan was a well-respected man, one who was born and raised in Las Vegas. He was a real Nevadan, if there was such a thing.

His power out lived his own life. Years after his death, people were still haunted by Stan and his aggressive nature of rule, Mary held on to that for as long as she could. Then, once Mary passed away, the case was destined to be closed, forever.

Bill filled in a few details that Ray did not know, but there was nothing earth-shattering that raised a concern with Ray about Serina. He needed something more, something that would give him some insight as to who Serina really was, and what she wanted with Charlie. He knew his hunch was not enough to persuade Charlie, so he kept digging. Ray made another call to John Sittner. John was the first and foremost expert on personal history. Back in 1983, John founded a company called Ancestry.com. Ancestry was created to be a genealogical company that could track down someone's genetic genealogy and with all that information at his fingertips, he quickly became a historical expert in people. He was often called to testify on behalf of the State of Nevada to determine the origin or lineage of a person's history for estate purposes or as a way to identify who was the next of kin. Consulting for the Las Vegas Police Department and University of Nevada, Las Vegas, there was no one better than John to dig up information that no one else could. Not only could he tell you where your family originated from or what your genealogy was, but he was able to find parents of missing children or the missing children of parents. He had a vast network of databases with everything from family history to personally identifiable information. John lived in Las Vegas, but would be called upon by government agencies, state departments or even foreign heads of state to help solve murders, crimes or just to help locate a person of interest.

Although Ray's request was not needing a great deal of research or investigation, John would be able to provide the most accurate and detailed history on the Mary Rothwell. No matter who you were or where you lived, John could find you and your family. Ray was only concerned about one aspect, and that was the offspring of Peter and Mary. It took John a matter of hours to return the information to Ray. Peter and Mary had two children, a boy and a girl. The boy was firstborn and named Jacob. He was born eight years before the death of Peter. Three years after Peter had disappeared, Jacob was killed in a car accident; Mary was the driver. The other child was a girl. She was born five years prior to the disappearance of Peter. She was daddy's little girl and her name was Serina. After the trial and finding the body of Peter, and with Jacob's death, Mary coveted Serina's relationship. Serina was watched over closely, and not able to do what most of her friends did. Mary did everything she could to protect the only thing left in her life. The loss of a husband was devastating enough. With the loss of her firstborn and only son, Mary felt threatened and alone. She had no one to protect her and began to withdraw from friends and any other family she had left. Growing up and marrying Peter, Mary had been a very subservient wife. Peter was the man of the house, and she did what he asked. On the outside, Peter and Mary were partners and equal, but at home, Mary was not the strongest person. She enjoyed doing everything for the family and making sure Peter was happy, but after the death of her husband, Mary reinvented herself, she had no other option. She became a dictator with an iron hand and wanted to control everything in her life. Serina was all that she had left. Serina was the closest living thing she had to remembering Peter, and she would never let Serina out of her sight. Mary began to groom her only child.

Ray had known that Serina was the child of Mary and Peter Rothwell, but now he had proof, although she had already told Charlie who her father was, Ray was gathering enough proof to satisfy Charlie.   Ray was still working on getting more information on Serina, but he needed to still determine why she showed up, appearing to hunt Charlie. Little did Ray know that Charlie was on a weeklong trip with Serina and left no forwarding telephone numbers. Ray called Charlie's phone, but it went straight to voicemail. Ray then called Charlie's office and spoke to Doris. Doris was given strict instructions not to divulge Charlie's location, not to anyone. If there was a need to contact him, Charlie would call once a day to check messages and resolve any concerns. Doris did not tell Ray were Charlie was; only

that he was out for the week, and it was only Monday.

Ray told Doris to take a message and have Charlie call

him as soon as he could.

Tuesday

Charlie and Serina were just landing in Brazil.

Spending time on the beach in Rio de Janeiro and

Copacabana was just what the doctor ordered. Far

enough away from those who knew them and away

from all the distractions, so they could focus on them.

No office calls, no meetings, and no one telling them

what they should or shouldn't be doing. Charlie's

cottage was right on the ocean, overlooking the

Copacabana Beach, on a section of the beach that was

private. They were picked up at the airport by a limo

which took them directly to the first bar they saw for a

drink and then off to the residence. The cottage was

6500 square feet with the entire backside facing the beach. The backside of the property was constructed with all glass and a sweeping deck that expanded the entire length of the house. The deck was massive. There was a complete set of furniture, with a wet bar, built-in Weber barbeque, and small refrigerator. On each side of the deck were spiral staircases that led down to the private beach, covered with white fine sand. The cottage was sitting on five acres, with thick foliage and tropical trees separating them from the nearest neighbor.

The second story was the master bedroom, which had a wonderful view of the sunrise over the water. Included in the master suite was a full workout room, sauna, sitting area, along with a complete kitchen. The master suite had two double-sided fireplaces, one next to the bed and the other overlooking the master bathtub. On the lower level were four additional bedrooms each with their own private bathroom, a full kitchen, den and dining room, a separate office, a movie theater that could seat 25, and a game room. The housekeeper's quarters were separate from the main cottage. The entire cottage was a 'smart house' and all you had to do was speak. When you walked into a room, the lights would dim, or the temperature would be adjusted based on your preference.

On the way to the cottage, Charlie wanted to pick up the conversation with Serina, but he was waiting until they could be alone without any interruptions.

Upon arrival, Charlie and Serina headed for the beach to watch the sunset. He put his arms around her as they laid in the sand with her head buried in his chest. The glow of the sun slowly disappeared as it was engulfed by the distant water. The intense red circle painted the landscape with an orange hue as the reflection dissipated into the ocean waves. When they returned to the cottage, all their belongings had been unpacked and hung in the master closet. Fresh fruit and flowers filled the cottage as Chef Gabriele prepared dinner.

After a quick shower and change of clothes, they went down to dinner. A table that could seat twelve, had two place settings. The candles were lit, and the wine was chilling as Charlie and Serina took their seats. The smell coming from the kitchen was overwhelming as it made its way into the dining room. Dinner was started with warm towels to clean the face and hands, followed by a glass of water to cleanse the pallet. Charlie and Serina barely spoke a word to each other during dinner, it was just that amazing. Even though very little was said, the look in each other's eyes was enough to say that they wanted to be nowhere else but right here. Serina got up from the table and turned to head upstairs to the bedroom. Charlie stood by the table with a smile, and felt this was a good time to pick up on the conversation from a few days earlier.

"Before we head up, can we talk for a minute?" Charlie asked.

"Of course. What did you have in mind?" Knowing exactly what Charlie had in mind, Serina responded.

Serina came back to the table and took her seat next to Charlie. Feeling nervous, Charlie could not hold back any longer.

"I wanted to pick back up on our conversation from a few days ago, when you came home. Why are you here? Why did you come back? And I guess, if we wanted to start at the beginning, why me?" Charlie stared off without the softball questions.

"Were do you want me to start?" Serina asked.

"Start at the beginning. You show up, basically from out of nowhere, and it feels like you had a purpose or plan. What are the chances that you show up in Tahoe, and we happen to meet at a restaurant that I frequent often and you find me, knowing what I drive and where I eat."

Serina pulled back her hands from the table and put them in her lap. Looking Charlie in the eyes, she began her response.

"It was not random. I did come to Tahoe for a reason," Serina paused.

Charlie sat there, observing her body language and see that she was uncomfortable, he waited.

"I came to Tahoe for you. To hurt you."

Silence filled the room. Charlie leaned in, with chills running down his spine.

"You came to hurt, me? Why?"

With tears forming in her eyes, Serina took Charlie's hand.

"My parents were friends of your parents, but I think you already knew that. When my mom died, I was so angry. Feelings from my past began to surface and I was mad, anxious and remembered everything my mom had told me years ago."

"Yes, I know my parents knew yours. But that does not explain why you came to find me and why you were or are so angry."

"For years, my mom had been telling me that it was your parents who were involved in my father's disappearance. He was murdered. My mother said it was because of your family. She had kept pictures of your parents and of you. She told me everything there was to know about you."

"Ok, that seems a little strange. I had heard that your father was murdered, and I also heard that there was someone who was convicted of this. I am so sorry about your father, I really am, but my parents or me, didn't have anything to do with that. So again, why me?"

"I was raised thinking that it was you, who I needed to find and have you pay for what happened to my father. I came to Tahoe for revenge Charlie."

Charlie stood up from the table and rubbed his mouth. Looking around to see if there was anyone else in the room, Charlie continued the conversation, knowing that Serina was visibly upset.

"And now? How are you feeling right now? Do you still want to hurt me, for something I had no idea about? Something that my family had no idea about?"

Serina got up from her seat and took Charlie's

hand.

"My whole life, I feel like I was raised for one purpose. And that was to find you and hurt you. I love you Charlie and I can't imagine hurting you. I see what an amazing life we can have, and I want that with you." Serina said as she kissed his hand.

Not knowing how to respond, Charlie took Serina by the hand and they walked upstairs.

"Thank you for being honest with me. I know it was not easy, but we are grown adults. No matter what our parents did, that does not have to destroy what we have and what we can have. This makes me a little uncomfortable, but we want to create this amazing life together, we can't have any distractions. This is you and I now, no one else can make us do something, we don't want to do." Charlie explained as they reached the bedroom.

"How about a dip in the pool?" He said.

Serina smiled and changed her direction towards the heated beach pool that was complete with LED lights, a water fountain, and a floating island.

Serina kissed Charlie on the lips and said thank you.

"Thank you for listening Charlie. Do you have any other questions?"

"Not right now. I think that is enough talk for one night. Can we just try and look forward, no looking back? We only have us to look forward to." Charlie said as he took off his shirt.

Serina took off her clothes and ran into the pool. Charlie watched as she disappeared into the steamy water, moonlight reflecting off the aqua blue surface. Charlie soon followed, throwing his pants to the side and walking in slowly. Dipping under the water and making his way towards Serina and resurfacing right

behind her. Easing her into the side of the pool from

behind, he reached his hand around to her face and

pulled it in close. Kissing her lips, he lowered his hand

to her stomach, feeling her abdomen tighten with

anticipation. Ever so gently, biting her shoulder, Serina

rolled her head back as she looked up at the stars above.

The lights from the pool lit up the night sky as a fog

completely covered the pool from the water mixed with

cool light flowing air. Coming in from behind, he could

feel how tight she was. Slowly with a gentle force, he

pushed up against her bottom, getting deeper and

deeper with every thrust. He could hear her moan and

let out a whispering breath of discomfort.

"Do you want me to stop?" he said into her ear.

"No, go deeper," she responded.

Charlie could feel every bit of himself inside her.

Squeezing her nipples between his fingers, he continued to push his body into hers.

"Right there, right there." She said as she reached her climax.

Carrying Serina and her weightless body to the sandy beach entrance of the pool, Charlie laid her back down and got on top of her. With the sand and water covering them all over, Charlie pushed harder and harder. Serina climaxed once again. This time Charlie was not able to hold back and let everything go. He could feel the sensation flowing out of himself, his heart was racing fast.   Charlie had never made love in a pool before, but he was getting use to the idea and liked it very much. Serina laid motionless as Charlie buried his head into the sand in exhaustion. Getting up and brushing the sand from each other's bodies, Serina asked, "Are you coming to bed?"

"It's not time for bed just yet." Charlie replied, taking her hand and leading her out to the patio.

The night air was cool as they made their way through the glass French doors. Serina saw two massage tables set up with robes draped over each one. Charlie and Serina's night ended with an oil massage and facial. No sex, no foreplay, just sleep, which was the only thing on in their minds after completing their rub down.

Being only Tuesday, Ray called again and spoke to Doris about Charlie. Doris sat there and listened to what Ray had to say. Although Charlie did not call in that day, Doris assured Ray that she would let Charlie know that he called, and that was the end of the conversation. After she hung up the phone, Doris was growing more concerned with each day, fearing for Charlie, but not sure why. It was true that she had a funny feeling about Serina the first time around, but never gave it much thought. Now that Ray had shared

some of the facts, Doris grew uneasy about this new

relationship. Ray told Doris that he and Charlie had a

conversation about his parents and that they had done

something that may come back to haunt Charlie. He also

said that Serina was the daughter of a parent who was

murdered and that she was there to get revenge on

Charlie. Doris knew Ray well and he was not the kind of

person to get overly concerned unless there was

something to be concerned about. With every new

conversation with Ray, Doris was growing equally

apprehensive about the situation. Doris rang Charlie,

but went straight to voicemail. She wanted Charlie

home and away from Serina before anything bad

happened. She could not leave that exact message on his

phone, but would try calling again in an hour.

Ray was not a quitter. If Ray knew something

was wrong, he would stop at nothing to figure it out. It was Tuesday evening at 7:15, and he was on his way to the airport to catch a plane to Tahoe to save Charlie. Doris never told Ray where Charlie was, but he wanted to be closer just in case anything happened. Whatever it took, Ray was going to confront Charlie and tell him to leave Serina. Since Charlie was not answering his phone, Ray felt face to face, is how this needed to go down. Ray was still collecting more information on Serina, but he knew enough to know that Charlie was in danger.

Ray rushed to the airport for the next flight to Lake Tahoe.

Wednesday

Awoken by the ringing of the breakfast bell, Charlie and Serina got out of bed and made their way downstairs, it was 9:00 am. Breakfast was already on the table and consisted of a variety of fresh fruit, orange and apple juice and a bagel with cream cheese. Something light to help them reach their next destination. Their plans were to be at the plane by 12:00 that afternoon and head for the Panama Canal. Eating did not take long, as they headed back upstairs to pack and get ready for their next journey. By the time they got upstairs from eating, their clothes were already packed and the suitcases were heading downstairs. Charlie reached the top of the stairs and went to the balcony to look one last time at the ocean view. Serina followed behind and put her arms around Charlie's chest and laid her head onto his back. Charlie turned around and kissed Serina just as a tear came out of her eye. He reached up with his right hand and wiped the tear and kissed her check.

"Everything all right?"

"Yes, I think so. I'm confused inside. A part of

me wants to be angry at you, but I have gotten to know who you are, and that just makes me sad. I want to enjoy all this, and I am trying." Serina responded.

"What were you expecting? I can give you anything you want. I can give you the world. Forget what brought you to me, and look around. This is the life I want to give you. The past, is in the past. It is just you and I now and we can make of this whatever we want. If you are conflicted or confused, maybe now is not the right time for us?" Charlie said.

"I want to make this work. I love you and in my heart, it hurts how much I love you. My mind is all over the place."

"What are you saying? I feel this way, Serina, I love you. There has never been another woman who makes me feel the way you do. When I first saw you, I wanted to be with you. I get that same feeling today, right now. You make me nervous; you make the palms

of my hands sweat. You make me feel more alive than

anything I have ever done. You give me this feeling that

I have never felt before. One of excitement and mystic,

one that I never got even when meeting with billionaires.

You do this to me. You are everything I ever imagined a

woman to be. You are beautiful, you have a wonderful

smile, you have melting eyes, and you are who you are.

I don't want to spend any more time alone, and I don't

think you do either."

Before Charlie could finish his last line, Serina

ran into the back room of the house and closed the door.

Charlie stood out on the balcony, looking into the sun.

He had just poured his heart out. He'd said things to

Serina, that he thought he would never say or feel.

Charlie walked back into the house and knocked on the

bedroom door. There was no answer. Again, Charlie

knocked on the door.

Finally, Serina answered and let Charlie in.

"I'm sorry, but last night was hard. Having to remember those days and why I am here, or at least why I was here. What you said, I wasn't expecting it. I was not prepared to fall in love with you, that was never the plan." Serina said.

"Help me understand what that means. Do you want to leave?"

"No, not at all. It was beautiful. No one has ever said what you said to me before. I don't want this to end and no, I am not going anywhere, except with you."

"Are you sure? I don't want to put you in an uncomfortable place. I want this to feel natural, just as it does for me. I want you to get nervous when you see me, I want your heart to beat with anticipation and love with just the mention of my name, because that's what happens to me. I will do whatever you want, you just need to say what that is. We both need to move on from what our parents may or may not have done to each other. You just need to trust me and I will need to trust you. With what you said last night, I am a little nervous and scared. I must be mad trying to keep you in my life when you told me you want to hurt me, but here I am. I am not going anywhere as long as you tell me we are alright."

Serina looked into Charlie's eyes and kissed his lips, turned around and left the room. Charlie followed. He was not stupid, but he was letting his heart rule his mind. Charlie knew this was a warning, but he felt he could change her. If Serina could see the real Charlie, and what he could provide to her, he wanted to change her mind.

"Are you coming?" She said from outside the

doorway.

"Yes, I'm coming."

The plane was ready when Charlie and Serina boarded. There was lite music on in the background and a movie was playing on the screen, *An Officer and a Gentlemen*. Charlie's plane is only two years old. Unlike his other aircraft, this one he ordered directly from Boeing and was involved throughout the entire interior build process. If there was an option, he had to have it. It had the room to seat up to 15 people in the main cabin. In the middle of the plane was the entertainment center complete with a 60-inch LED television, DVD, surround sound with ten speakers built into the walls and floor of the plane, a complete interactive stereo/computer system with a tuner, 30 band equalizer, CD/CD-ROM and internet connection with a separate 30-inch screen. This enabled Charlie to work from his plane just as if he was in his office. He could log onto the internet and connect to the cloud to access any of his client files. The end of the plane had two bedrooms each with its own bathroom. Both came complete with a king size bed, a small entertainment center with surround sound and a Jacuzzi. The plane cost Charlie 60 million dollars and he paid in cash.

Ray's plane landed at three in the morning on Wednesday. Flying into Reno on a redeye was nothing new for the second city that does not sleep in Nevada. When Ray comes to visit Charlie, he usually lands at the Lake Tahoe airport, but this time, not knowing where Charlie was, he flew into Reno. The airport was packed with visitors and potential gamblers. Ray caught an Uber to the Eldorado Hotel and Casino Resort. One of the nicer places in the area, Ray did not have a problem getting a room. Since he only needed it for a few hours,

Ray went upstairs and crashed on the bed. He needed

his sleep for the ride up to Tahoe and his adventure in

finding Charlie.

The morning came quick for Ray especially when

one drinks a fifth of Southern Comfort just for bedtime.

His body got him up at 4:30 and he could not fall back

asleep. He went down to the casino and played some

blackjack where he won $500. With his winnings, he

went to the bar and persuaded the tender to sell him a

bottle of Southern Comfort for $50. Ray then proceeded

up to his room and drank the bottle, he fell fast asleep.

Southern Comfort was his melatonin. A knock at the

door woke up Ray at 10:00, it was housekeeping.

Jumping into a shower and put his belongings in his bag,

Ray called room service for some breakfast and aspirin.

Ray checked out of the hotel and rented a Chevy

Tahoe so that he could drive up the mountain to warn

his friend. On the way, Ray called Bill for an update on Serina. Bill had some interesting news to share.

"Bill, it's Ray, heading up to the lake to see Charlie, but wanted to see if you had anything else on Serina?"

"Hope you had a safe trip. I actually do have some new details to share with you. I did some more digging into her mom, Mary, and who she called or hung out with before she died. She became close friends with a woman named Rose Betrise. Rose also has a daughter who is the same age as Serina, so they too became friends. I spoke to Rose yesterday, and she was very forthcoming with information. And honestly, if it was not for you even asking about this, we would have never been able to find this information. I have opened a case here in Clark County, and have been in contact with the Washoe County, El Dorado County and Placer

County Sheriff's department. I think you have led us to discover a plan that has yet to happen. It sounds like this Mother Mary was a great teacher."

"Teacher? I don't understand."

"Mary apparently confided in Rose about the death of Peter, and who she thought was to blame. Until the day she died, Mary claimed that it was Charlie's parents who killed him. She told Rose that she would get Charlie, if it was the last thing she did on this earth. Well, of course she was not capable of getting to Charlie, but she raised, trained, and taught the next best thing. That's right; Serina. Rose said that Mary was coaching and training Serina to get to Charlie and dispose of him, just as they had done to her husband. At first, I thought the whole plot of revenge was a little off, coming from Rose, who is in her 70's. But then I talked to her daughter, Kathleen."

"Are you telling me that Mary raised Serina for the sole purpose of seeking revenge for the death of her husband, by doing something to Charlie? What could they possibly do to Charlie? And why does she think his parents had anything to do with his death?"

"According to Kathleen, Serina was going to Tahoe to look for Charlie. She was going to 'get involved' in his life and turn it upside down. Mary and Serina apparently have done their research on your buddy Charlie. They seemed to know everything about this guy. Serina often bragged about Charlie; all his houses or cars that he drove, how much money he had and how she was going to 'thoroughly' enjoy taking all that away. From what Kathleen said Ray, Serina's plan has always been to kill Charlie. She never said how she would do it, but only that that was her sole purpose. Kathleen never thought too much of it, and thought it was all just talk." Bill said to silence on the other end.

Ray always suspected something was amiss with Serina, that is why he flew out to Tahoe, but never in his dreams did he ever think something of this magnitude. Ray had seen Serina only once, and from that one look, what could a woman of her size do to a man like Charlie? Whatever it was, Serina was raised to do one particular job, and it was up to Ray to stop her. Ray hung up the phone and tried calling Charlie on his cell phone, but again, it went straight to voicemail. Ray's uneasy feelings towards Serina were spot-on. She could not be trusted, and Ray felt horrible that he was right.

It was 1:00 in the afternoon by the time Ray walked into Rocklin and Roll Investments, Inc. Doris greeted him as he approached Charlie's office.

"Ray, what a surprise to see you in Tahoe. What, are you doing here? You know Charlie is not here this week."

"Doris, how are you? Yes, I know he is not here, but do you know where he is? I need to get a hold of him immediately." Ray said.

Ray asked Doris to open the door to Charlie's office so he could try and find something. Not sure what, but he needed to keep himself busy otherwise he was going to hurt something. He was mad, he was upset, he wanted to hurt Serina. He started going through papers and drawers to look for clues as to where Charlie and Serina were. Charlie made sure that no one knew about this trip, and Doris only knew because Charlie told her everything. No one else in the office or even business partners knew where Charlie was. Ray kept looking and yelled for Doris. Doris came in and closed the door behind her.

"Doris, you really need to tell me where they are.

Charlie is in danger, serious danger, like life danger,"
Ray said trying to be slightly vague.

"What do you think you are doing here? I know
you and Charlie are good friends, but is this how you
treat a good friend? Why don't you trust him, why don't
you trust her?" Doris said, equally as concerned, but
wanted to see if she could get any more details from Ray.

"It is not that I don't trust Charlie, I can't trust
Serina." Ray could not hold back any longer.

"She is going to kill him. She is going to do
something to Charlie, Doris. Do you realize how
important it is that we get a hold of him right now? I
have some information that Charlie needs to know
about. I'm telling you that his life is in danger. She is
fucking mental." Ray tried to explain using as few words
as possible.

"Ray, I don't understand. How do you know

this?" Doris said.

"Why do you think I came all the way out here? I'm not here on a frequent flyer pass. I need to get a hold of Charlie. Serina is out to get him. She thinks Charlie's parents killed her father. She was raised by her mother to seek revenge by hurting Charlie. Her plan is to get him away from everyone and kill him."

Ray talked as he took a seat. Feeling his heartbeat through his neck, Ray took a deep breath and continued.

"I talked to the sheriff in Vegas, and they have alerted the police here. I got this information from an investigator in the department and then I talked to one of Serina's old neighbors. Apparently, Serina was raised by Mary, her mother, to find Charlie and make him pay for what she thinks Charlie's parents did to the dad."

Doris sat down in one of the office chairs and

started to cry. She was shaking and knew she had to tell

Ray where they were. She had met Serina, and a killer

seemed like the last thing she could be. She was a little

shy, but not a killer. Doris didn't want to believe it, but

knew she had no reason not to, based on what Ray was

telling her.

"OK, so what do we do? How can I help?"

Ray continued with his rant, as if he did not hear

a word Doris said. He was in a panic.

"Why do you think Serina disappeared last year?

Why did she pick up and just leave Charlie? Answer me

that. Remember how happy he was? His life was

making the full circle until he came home one day, and

she was gone. Gone for no reason at all? No, she was

gone because she was in the midst of her planning. I

don't know why she left when she did, but I can tell you

that I know why she came back."

"She was taking care of her father Ray. But you are saying that her father was murdered? Serina left to be by his side, that is what she told Charlie. He is sick, he is dying."

"Not dying Doris. He is definitely not dying; I can tell you that for certain. Serina's father, Peter, DIED thirty years ago!" Ray yelled.

There was silence in the air. Doris, shaking uncontrollably, sat down on the edge of the desk. Rubbing her hands together and wiping away tears, she talked to Ray.

"I actually do not know where Charlie is at the moment. I have no idea. I feel so guilty letting him go away without trying to stop him." Doris said as she continued to cry in fear.

"What do you mean you don't know where he is?"

"He calls every day, just once, to check in, but he did not call yesterday. Charlie did not call! Oh my god, do you think something happened to him?" Tears began streaming from her face.

"I don't know; I really don't know. Can you please look around or try and find out where he is? Can you check the last place they were?"

Doris tried calling Charlie's phone, but it kept ringing. No answer. She hung up and tried again. Voice mail full. She then tried the plane, but again, no answer. Doris was still shaking uncontrollably and had to sit down. Ray came up behind her, and put his hand on her shoulder.

****

Just as the plane was landing in Costa Rica, Charlie called the office to check messages and see how Doris was getting along without him. Much to his surprise, Doris did not answer the phone.

"Hello?"

"Hello, this is Charlie Rocklin, who is this?"
Charlie said to the male voice on the other end.

"This is Ray, and we need to fucking talk man.
Where are you?"

"Ray, what are you doing in Tahoe? What are
you doing answering my phone? I did not know you
were going to be up for a visit. Where is Doris?"

"You have lots of questions for someone who is
in trouble. I also have questions, but they seem more
like the answers. I'm not here for a social visit, I came
here to save you. You are in danger, serious danger.
You need to come home, tonight! Like get on your plane
and come home right now." Ray tried to speak in a calm
yet determined demeanor.

"What is all this about? Please don't tell me it's

about Serina. I'm not going to listen to this if it is."

"Charlie, answer me this one question: Have you asked Serina why she left you six months ago?"

"Yes, I did."

"And what did she tell you?"

"She had to visit her father, who was very sick. But when I asked her about Peter Rothwell, she told me everything. She said that he was murdered and that she was coming to Tahoe to hurt me. She said her mother raised her to seek revenge because they think my father killed him."

Ray listened to what Charlie was saying and was having trouble finding the words to respond with. It was as if Charlie just knocked the wind out of his sails. And if that was the case, why would Charlie still be with this person, who admittingly, wants to hurt him.

"Jesus, what is wrong with you people? Yes, that

is exactly what I was going to tell you. She actually told you that?"

"Yes, she told me everything."

"I have been talking to my buddy in the department down in Vegas and they have alerted the authorities up here. I talked to some of their old neighbors and that is true, Mary was raising Serina to get revenge. Even Serina was bragging about that to her neighbor friend Charlie, that she was going to find you and kill you. Does that not make you want to just run, come home man."

"Honestly yes, it does worry me some, but we have been talking and she confessed to me. She is not like that anymore. She is not going to do anything to me, trust me on this."

"Charlie, come on, you know who you are talking to. I have spent my life dealing with people just like Serina. They are not what they appear to be, or even what she is pretending to be. The evidence is overwhelming, and you are in danger my friend. She cannot be trusted, and I need you to come home so I can see you. I just want to see you."

"We are landing here in Costa Rico; we are planning on coming home tomorrow. Even after what I just told you, you think I'm still in danger? Ray, I trust you and I know you well enough to hear the concern in your voice, but we will be home tomorrow. Nothing is going to happen, no one is going to get hurt."

"Charlie, you need to trust me on this. I really think you need to just come home, tonight." Ray said as he was looking at Doris.

Putting the phone on mute, Ray talked to Doris.

"I'm trying, but he is just not listening. And she told him everything! She told him, she was raised to hurt him, and he still won't come home."

Taking the phone off mute, Ray continued.

"Are you going to come home tonight?"

"Come on, I'm thousands of miles away. To fly home tonight would be ridiculous. I think your cause for alarm is a bit exaggerated at this point. I already know. You can talk to me when I get back into town on Saturday night. Is Doris around?"

"Saturday, what happened to tomorrow? Saturday is three days from now. You could be dead in three days Charlie."

"Dead! Are you serious right now Ray? Saturday Ray, I will be home Saturday."

"She is going to kill you," Ray yelled into the phone, loud enough for everyone else on the floor to hear.

"Ok, I'm done here. I'm done listening to this.

Put Doris on the phone or the next thing you are going to hear is a dial tone."

Ray was at a complete and utter loss for words. What more could he say to convince Charlie? Ray was exhausted. He could not muster another word, and handed the phone to a crying Doris, who was standing right next to him.

"Charlie, are you alright?" Doris said trying to get the words out.

"Doris, yes, I'm fine. I know you must be worried, hearing all of this, but we can talk when I get back home. Everything is fine, I promise you."

"Charlie, I think you need to come home before Saturday. I have listened to what Ray told you and he is telling the truth. You need to come home, please."

"Doris, listen to me. I'm fine, and Serina is fine. We are going to finish up our trip and I will see you on

Monday morning. I will be in the office on Sunday to get my calendar ready for Monday. Don't worry about me and stop listening to Ray. I'm going to hang up now. I may not call again, so I'll see you when I get there." And Charlie hung up.

Charlie got off the phone and threw it across the plane. It hit the window and fell to the ground. He shook his head and ran both hands through his hair. Serina came in from the main cabin and sat next to Charlie. She put her arms around him and laid her head on his shoulder.

"Is everything alright?" Serina asked.

"Yes, no. But it will be. They are just worried about me."

"Because of me?"

"Yes, because of you. They think you are going to hurt me to get back at my parents. My parents had

nothing to do with your father, I want you to know that."
Charlie said.

"I'm sorry you are going through this. Is there
anything I can do?"

"Are you going to hurt me?" Charlie asked,
looking at Serina.

With a smile, Serina kissed Charlie on the lips and
rubbed his face.

"We already talked about this. I am not who I
was Charlie." Serina said.

"You didn't answer the question."

"About me hurting you? I told you; I am not
who I was."

Charlie swallowed hard and tried to take a deep
breath. He felt as if he was suffocating from the inside.
The air was all around him, but he could not breathe it
in. Serina did not answer the question or could not.

Charlie was nervous. He couldn't focus; his vision was

suddenly blurred. Charlie turned away from Serina and

headed for the pilot. Just as Sam was preparing to

disembark the plane, he gave the order.

"Sam, I'm sorry, but can you please take us

home. We really need to leave, now."

"Yes sir. I just need to make sure we have

enough fuel, and we'll be on our way."

****

Frustrated with the way the conversation went,

Ray headed for Rotchedo's for a drink. It was early

evening. Ray called Frankie from the car and was

greeted as he walked into the restaurant. A table and a

drink were waiting in the back of the restaurant

overlooking the lake. There could not be a more

enjoyable place to enjoy a drink and look out onto the

glistening water of Lake Tahoe. There were small ripples from the brief gusts of wind that filled the basin.

Frankie and Ray shook hands, and sat at the table, talking. Ray did not hold anything back. He was upset, he wanted to scream, but instead, he talked to Frankie. He told Frankie all about Serina and her parents. Ray talked about Charlie's parents, their relationship with the Rothwell's, and how they met. He talked about the murder of Peter, and how Mary raised Serina for revenge. He showed Frankie all the information Bill had sent him. Frankie was speechless. Never in a million years did he ever suspect Serina would do something like this. He did not know Serina very well, but revengeful was the last thing that came to mind. Frankie was also very protective of Charlie, just like Ray. After an hour, Frankie's head was exploding with information. He needed to hear Charlie's voice.

Frankie got up from the table and went to the

phone to call Charlie's house, but Charlie did not answer. He called Charlie's cell, but Charlie did not answer. Ray had told him that Charlie was not home, but Frankie was in a panic and tried every number he had. Next, he called Doris at home, and she relayed the same information Ray did. Doris began crying again. Frankie called the house again, and Brian answered.

"Brian, this is Frankie, do you know where Charlie is?"

"Charlie is away and will be returning within the next two days."

"I need to get a hold of him right now. He is in danger, and I need to talk to him. Do you know where he is?"

"Frankie, I truly do not know where Charlie is; he didn't divulge that information to me, perhaps Doris may know." Brian replied.

"Brian, do me this one favor, call here at the

restaurant when Charlie arrives. Right when you see him, call me and I will come to the house. If you cannot reach me here, call my cell phone. This is very important. Can you do that for me?"

"Yes. You can count on it."

"And Brian, do not tell Charlie, just call me, understand?"

"Yes, I'll call you when I know that Charlie is home."

Ray and Frankie continued to talk into the night awaiting the call from Brian. The chances of Brian calling here are pretty slim based on Ray's last conversation with Charlie. He was not planning on returning home until Saturday and it was only Wednesday. They were out of options; they could not get to Charlie. The only hope was that Charlie would come to his senses, listen to what Ray had told him, and come home early, without alarming Serina. It was now a waiting game. Frankie and Ray continued talking. What was their plan? Even if Brian did call, what could they really do?

Frankie called some police buddies from the Placer County Sherriff's department and asked that they come down to the restaurant. He called Bobby, Mike and Phillip, who were already aware of the case, thanks to Bill. The three arrived within fifteen minutes, dressed for battle, followed by several other police cars. The clock was approaching midnight, and the nine men were talking and drinking at the bar, awaiting that one phone call. One suggested to go to the house, but they knew if Serina saw one of the cars or had any idea, she would likely take Charlie somewhere else. The only option was to wait.

Thursday

As the clock in the main room of Rotchedo's struck two a.m., Bobby, Mike and Phillip got an emergency call.

"Listen Frankie, you know how to reach us. We are not far away, there is a reported shooting, and we have to take the call. The others will stay here with you. When you hear something, call us, we will come down. Do not go to the house alone, we can handle that. If what we have is correct, we have authority and priority and will be right here," Mike said to Frankie.

"Guys, thank you for coming down. I have no idea when Charlie will be coming back to town, but when I hear, you will be the first I call. I owe you guys big for this, thanks."

"You owe us nothing. Charlie is like family, and no one fucks with our family."

As the three walked out, Ray shook his head and got up from the table to walk around.

"This is fucking ridiculous. Where is Charlie,

and why can't anyone get a hold of him. God damnit, this is killing me. We should just go to the house. Charlie will need us if he ever gets there," Ray yelled.

"There is nothing we can do right now. It's two in the morning, what do you want to do? We should not go to the house; you heard Mike. Plus, I doubt these guys would even let us leave. If Serina does know we are there, she could do something, and we could lose him forever."

"Frankie, can I crash here? You go on home, I need to stay here, close to the house in case the call comes in. I have a feeling that Charlie is coming home."

"Fuck that, Ray. You and I both will be staying here. Charlie is my brother, man. I am sure as shit not going anywhere until I know where he is and that he is safe. There is a sofa bed in my office, you can stay on that. I am not sure I can sleep right now. I will just sit

right here with my Blanton's." Frankie responded,
raising his glass.

3:30 a.m.

The night sky was clear as can be with a cold chill
in the air. As Charlie's plane was making its final decent
to the Tahoe airport, Ray was laying quietly on the sofa.
Frankie was just finishing his bottle of Blanton's, eyes
wide open.

"Frankie, you awake?"

"Yep, no sleeping here."

"I have a feeling man, Charlie is close."

"I hope you're right man; I hope you're right," he
said, taking the last sip of his drink.
The restaurant was silent and still. You could hear the
sound of distant waters crashing on to the beach.

Charlie's plane stopped inside the hanger, and
the doors opened as Charlie and Serina stepped out and

headed for his Aston Martin that was parked inside. Not a word was spoken, not a look was given. The only thing Charlie told Serina was that they had to return home because of an emergency call from Doris, no other explanation was provided. Charlie opened the passenger door and closed it behind Serina as she got in. Living only five minutes away from the airport had its advantages, especially tonight, but it felt like an hour. Charlie and Serina did not say a word to each other. By the time they arrived at the house, it was now four in the morning. Charlie parked the car in the garage and closed the door behind them. He dropped the bags by the door and invited Serina in as he headed for the bedroom, taking off his shirt, exhausted. He knew he was safe, now that he was back in his own house.

"Are you not going to ever talk to me again?" Serina asked.

"Serina, I love you. I would give anything to you, but I don't believe you. There is something wrong here. You tell me you came here to hurt me, then we have a great time together and you can't even answer a question on how you are feeling now. I don't want to be with someone thinking they are going to do something to me when I turn around. You frighten me, or the idea of what you might do, frightens me." Charlie said as he reached the bedroom. Serina was looking at Charlie, but didn't say anything.

Charlie went into the bedroom and Serina turned the other way and headed for the kitchen. The house was dark, and the marble tile leading to the kitchen was cold. Charlie turned on his phone and was inundated with missed calls and text messages. He called Ray. No answer. Ray's eyes had grown heavy, and he was sleeping on the sofa. His phone was buried deep in his pocket. While Frankie was still sitting at the bar, he did not hear the ring.

Serina walked slowly into the kitchen and noticed the light on in Brian's room. She could hear the TV as she put her ear to the door. Cracking the door just enough to look inside, she could see Brian asleep in bed. Leaving the door cracked, Serina went into the kitchen and opened the top drawer to get a large carving knife. She put it behind her as she went back to Brian's room, where he was lying on his side. Serina approached the bed and took a pillow that was on the corner chair. She placed the pillow over Brian's head and drove the knife through the pillow, into his skull. He did not move or make a sound. Serina checked her hands to make sure they were still clean. She raised her hand in the air and saw that it was disturbingly steady. She left the room and closed the door behind her, leaving the light of the

TV reflecting off the blade that remained in Brian's lifeless body.

Serina walked back into the kitchen to get another knife. Cautiously walking back to the bedroom, she could hear Charlie finishing in the shower. Before Charlie ends each shower, he blows his nose. Serina stepped to Charlie's side of the bed and placed the knife under the mattress. Charlie got out of the shower, dried himself off and crawled into bed. Serina walked into the closet and emerged holding a short red dress with white lace trim, and laid it on the end of the bed.

"What are you doing?" Charlie asked.

"Just getting my clothes ready for morning," she said in a low, somber voice.

Seeing the dress, Charlie looked at Serina. Squinting his eyes, and staring at the dress once again, he knew that dress. He was trying to think where he had seen it before, but he could not place it. Dark images of a shadowy woman appeared in the back of Charlie's mind, wearing that same dress. The woman in the parking garage. Charlie was sleepy, his eyes were struggling to keep open, but the sight of the dress got him to sit up.

"Is that new?" he asked.

"No, I've had it awhile." Serina said without looking at Charlie.

Charlie was uneasy. Feeling the tension in the room, he could not fall asleep. He watched Serina's every move.

Serina looked at Charlie in bed and made her way towards him. She removed her clothes, dropped them to the floor, and turned around to take a shower. Charlie watched as she got in and watched her wash her body and hair. He was mad, he was angry, and he truly didn't know who this person was, but he couldn't control himself; he had to look. Her beauty blinded him every time.

Charlie picked up his phone and called Ray again. Still no answer, but he left a message.

"Ray, I am home, and Serina is here. Not sure where you are man, but I need you here." Charlie said as he was still struggling with his feelings for Serina.

The water turned off and Serina walked out of the shower, dripping wet, looking right at Charlie.

"Are you alright?" Serina said as she walked closer to the bed where Charlie was lying, leaving a trail of water behind her.

"I'm not sure. I need to think about this, about us." Charlie said.

"Can I give you something to think about?"

"Not tonight. We need to talk, but honestly, I'm

just too tired right now."

"We can talk in the morning Charlie," she said with a short but determined smile.

Serina climbed into bed with Charlie and started kissing his neck. Her hands moved up his leg and over his stomach, quivering with emotion. They continued to move up to his chest to his mouth, where she put her finger on his tongue. She began kissing and biting his nipples and could feel Charlie getting hard.

At 4:45, Ray woke up and checked his phone. He noticed a missed call from Charlie and called out to Frankie, who was finishing his second bottle.

"Frankie, let's go! Charlie called."

"What did he say, is he alright?"

"I must have fallen asleep; I missed his call. We have to go."

"Call him back." Frankie said in a fast, directive

order.

"No, I told him to call when he got home. I don't want to give Serina any indication that we're here. He left a message saying he is home. Call Mike."

In the car on the way to Charlie's, Frankie called Mike to have them meet at the house. "They're on their way."

Charlie pulled Serina up, rolled her over on her stomach, and made his way on top of her. He positioned her legs so he could enter. Charlie's mind was in a frenzy. He could not think straight, and thoughts were bombarding him. As Charlie moved, Serina turned her head to look at Charlie. He was staring off and did not notice Serina looking at him. She could see that he was preoccupied and did not want to lose the moment. This was her moment. She pushed him over to his side of the bed and climbed on top of him. She leaned over to kiss his ear and guided their bodies together in motion. Serina could feel that he was getting close. She continued to move back and forth over Charlie as he closed his eyes.

Ray and Frankie drove up to the front of the house and got out of the car before it had even come to a full stop. Following close behind were three sheriff's deputy trucks. Mike and his fellow officers got out of their cars and joined Ray and Frankie at the front door. Looking inside, it was dark. Mike took out his Colt 45 and used the butt of the gun to break a small glass square on the front door, allowing him to get his arm through to unlock the door. There were no lights on in the house as the six sheriff deputies made their way inside, with Frankie and Ray close behind.

"Upstairs!" Frankie said as he pointed to the staircase.

Leaning down once again, she kissed his ear, and forced her breasts into Charlie's mouth. Reaching down to remove the knife from under the mattress, Serina's nipple was between Charlie's teeth. Holding the knife to the side, Serina grabbed a pillow that was next to Charlie's head. Holding the pillow tight with her left hand, she fiercely grabbed the knife in her right. As her heart rate began to increase with anticipation, she raised the pillow up slightly to slide over Charlie's head, whose eyes were still closed. Knowing he was thinking about something else; she raised the pillow a little more. Just as she took one last breath and began to say something, she noticed the movement on the security cameras. She could see the police cars outside of the house and others arriving.

Walking up the stairs with their guns drawn, Frankie motioned to the master bedroom. They could see a light on in the room.

Serina knew this was her only chance. She slid
the pillow over Charlie's face and brought forth the
knife. Just as she could feel Charlie's hands begin to rise,
she put her face on to the pillow and shouted, "this is for
my father!" and she drove the knife into the pillow,
feeling the resistance. As she forced the knife deeper,
Charlie's hands grabbed her sides, but he had no
strength. She twisted the knife into Charlie's neck as his
hands dropped to his side and his feet went limp.

Walking slowly through the doorway, guns in
the air, Mike took aim. Seeing Serina on top of Charlie in
bed, clinching the knife, Mike and two other deputies
opened fire. There was a barrage of bullets penetrating
Serina, throwing her body off the bed, slamming her into
the wall.

Ray and Frankie came running in and stopped as

they approached the end of the bed. Charlie was laying

there, with the knife sticking out of the pillow and a trail

of blood dripping on to the floor into a big pool. Charlie

was dead.

* 9 7 9 8 9 8 6 5 7 2 0 2 4 *